DELIA MEADE

DELIA MEADE

MARTIN KEAVENEY

PENNILESS PRESS PUBLICATIONS

www.pennilesspress.co.uk/books

Published by

Penniless Press Publications 2020

ISBN 978-1-913144-16-6

Cover Image: www.paulbutler.me

CONTENTS

To Bridget Mee

1.

Now the last of Delia Meade's many children have moved out, she decides to tackle the room under the stairs, known as the glory hole. The white door is not opened often and creaks as it comes out from the frame. Delia's eyes accustom to the darkness.

Slowly shapes become discernible. A line of human-like forms develops into the jackets her husband and sons wore. An oil lamp, three mangled coat hangers connecting bundles of electricity bills and a basket of empty jam jars hang from the underside of the stairs. Dark squares line the partition to the left. At the end, as the stairs leads to the floor, is an empty void.

Delia finds the switch on the wall. Light streams against the partition and the gable end, dust swirls as bands of dark shadows border the bright. She walks in, the outside fading behind her.

Delia pulls back the flaps of the first cardboard box. Within are clothes: woollen and cotton shapeless jumpers, torn stonewashed jeans, plain summer dresses, white working men's shirts. Another has miscellaneous objects: exotic statues, coverless books, USA biscuit tins with rattling contents. At the bottom, there is a cloth clad chest. She takes away the boxes above it, moving them toward the gable wall. She lifts the lid of the chest. A thick waft of dust and a damp musty smell rises.

There are many different items within: a brass jug, a shaving brush, a vinyl record with no label, a folded bundle of yellow papers in a thick elastic band, a dusty hardback book entitled *Construction Practices*, a doll whose mouth has fallen off. Only the holes left by the needle remain. She is on a road with her sister, the sun is shining. Everything is golden. There is a noise somewhere, her sister grabs her arm. Delia holds the doll for some moments.

Delia resumes taking out the objects, leaving them on the floor beside the chest. At the base are a pile of photographs. Some are in colour, curved at the corners, some black and white, others sepia toned or faded and indistinct.

Delia takes the bundle up, closes the lid and sits on top. She leafs through images of family occasions. One is a cutting from the parish magazine. A man stands at a fence, his hat awkwardly hooked on his head. There are rushes, gorse and murky pools in the background. Underneath the photograph is a caption which reads: 'Mr Flounders, 1926.'

A breeze lifts the stray hairs of Mr Flounders' moustache.

'Thank you, Mr Flounders,' the young man says, dismantling his apparatus.

Mr Flounders turns to the marshy ground behind the fence. Beyond the rushes is a dry gentle slope where young men kick a ball between wooden posts.

In Mr Flounders' vision, the shapes of people emerge, crowding at trails of stones, huddled together, wearing torn clothes, their voices following on for decades. His grandfather, cheeks red, walks with other men, pounding across the bog, roaring at the groups, crushing the morning silence.

Now Mr Flounders smiles. Houses would line each side of the area in front of him. In the middle, a good wide road for motor cars. The nearby football pitch would be a bonus. He takes out his pipe and lights it. A few people walk by, nodding at him, tipping their hat. 'Mr Flounders,' they say and he nods.

Delia can see a white corner peering out of Mr Flounders' left front jacket pocket, a piece of paper which outlines the steel and concrete specifications of a new type of house foundation. It was developed by a German and known as a 'raft' where the house above would float on the terrain. It allowed the construction of thousands of homes in marshy ground throughout Bavaria.

Delia looks closer at the area behind Mr Flounders on what was a dry and sunny day. At the end of the glory hole, something moves. Delia peers into the void.

The problems in the Bog Road during the building project were well discussed in houses, in front and back kitchens, in pubs and shops and on streets in the town over the years. The man from Germany had come and met Mr Flounders and checked the ground. He was a short thin man, with a narrow moustache and a grey jacket that shined in the light. He nodded as Mr Flounders explained his requirements. The German's assistant dug spade sized holes around the site and The German put down white sticks at various points.

Some months later, Mr Flounders arrived with a team of men. They had shovels and wheelbarrows and one hydraulic machine. They began to dig foundations for the houses on the Bog Road. The men shouted and laughed as they worked, their caps tweed and navy, their greatcoats spattered and creased, their smoking pipes long and curved.

One of the workers found a pile of bones within a square track of buried stone. They stacked all the bones together, in the centre of the site, until Mr Flounders could decide what to do with them. One of the men said the area was a graveyard, another did not think it was, his father had said it was an old village.

Mr Flounders told the men to throw the bones in a hole he had dug with the machine for dumping rubbish. The bones were heaped on top of cement packaging and waste steel and off cuts of timber.

One morning, some months into construction, Mr Flounders noticed one of the thresholds covered in a layer of torn peat and broken rushes. He asked the foreman and he did not know anything about it, so he asked the sub foreman and he did not know anything about it, so he asked one of the labourers and he did not know anything about it. Two of the men pulled a building line across the apex of the roofs. Twenty houses had sunk almost a foot. Mr Flounders sent word to Germany, but there was no reply to his telegram.

An engineer from the council, who were buying the houses from Mr Flounders, as long as they were not subterrain, said 'You'll have to knock them, I'm afraid.'

Mr Flounders had no insurance and there was nothing he could do, because he would not have enough money to knock them and build them again. His inherited land was a mess, twenty houses off level and sinking to where millions of ancient trees had sank before and built up layers of peat.

A lot of the men laughed over the ten o'clock break about the 'sinking houses,' and the 'mess,' it was and 'Sure who ever would build houses on bog, that was pure madness,' and 'See them bones. This place did them no good and it'll do Flounders no good now either.' They laughed again and smoked their long curving pipes and drank from whiskey bottles of sugared tea.

Mr Flounders came to work the next day at eight o'clock and walked up and down the new street past the twenty sinking houses. One had sunk more than the others. Mr Flounders went into this house and climbed the ladder to the first floor and took a thin rope from inside his jacket, tied it onto the roof joist and looped it around his neck. He stepped to the edge and jumped to the void between roof and floor. The rope cut into his skin and closed his windpipe, and Mr Flounders struggled as only the choking can and he tried to pull himself up the rope and reach for the safety of the floor above, which had seemed so close a moment earlier but his mind blanked and his eyes closed and the skin on his head went white. Delia looks up from the photograph, to the void and Frankie ran past her out of the glory hole to the back door.

All the sinking houses had to be knocked with sledges, and the rafts dug out, and the design revised with reinforced steel and concrete poured again and the houses rebuilt. Mr Flounders' wife wanted to call the street after her husband but that was overruled by the council.

Delia puts the cutting of Mr Flounders back on the pile. There is a bicycle spanner amongst the objects she took from the chest. She takes it up, feels the cold steel against her hands.

There is a knock on the door. The sound is of a low tap. If it were a salesman or a religious representative, the knock would be higher up, louder. This knock is timid, tapping slowly, seven to eight times within a few seconds.

Delia stands up, waddles out of the glory hole, through the back kitchen and down the front hall. She pulls back the safety chain and opens the front door, a shaft of light running across her face.

Mrs Freeley cuts a long thin silhouette against the daylight. A More cigarette burns in her left hand. She has a narrow face and is taller than Delia. Her knitted red cardigan is buttoned to the base of her lined neck. On her left shoulder hangs a cream handbag.

'How are you, dearie?' Mrs Freeley says, tossing the end of the cigarette on the path and crushing it with her light blue shoe.

They walk to the back of the house. Mrs Freeley continues through to the front kitchen. Delia stops in the back kitchen and takes the brown kettle off the cooker and half-fills it. She takes the large box of matches from the first press over the counter beside the cooker and lights the gas on the front left-hand hob. The blue flame flickers and she places the kettle over it. She arranges some arrowroot biscuits on a plate and carries them over to the round table in front of the tall window in the front kitchen.

When the kettle boils, Delia pours a small amount of water into the white delph teapot on the counter, swirling it around and pouring it down the sink. She puts in two teaspoons of tea leaves from a blue tin tea caddy with a picture of Captain Oates on the front and half-fills the teapot with the boiled water. She covers the teapot with a blue woollen tea cosy and brings it over to the round table.

Delia takes two cups and saucers from the first press over the counter beside the cooker and brings them over to the round table. The silver sugar bowl is already in the centre.

Delia sits on her armchair beside the red tiled mantelpiece in the front kitchen. The back of the armchair curves around her, ending with two cushioned armrests on either side, where she sometimes rests her forearms. She faces the tall window which looks out into the yard.

Mrs Freeley settles in the armchair opposite. She turns around and pours a cup of tea, adds some milk and stirs it with the teaspoon. She takes a biscuit in her left hand and turns back to the red tiled mantelpiece. When Mrs Freeley is finished, Delia gets up and pours her cup of tea, pours in her milk and takes one biscuit. She sits on her armchair. The fire crackles.

'Thank you, dearie,' Mrs Freeley says.

'How are you?'

'Good. It's a bit chilly.'

'It is for August, yes.'

The occasional spark flies over the black hearth and singes the brown patterned carpet. Delia and Mrs Freeley sit quietly for a time, looking ahead of themselves.

'Thomas is coming on Tuesday,' Delia says, eventually.

'Well, that's nice, dearie. How is he getting on in Dublin?'

'Not too bad, you know, work is up and down.'

'Oh indeed, indeed. Charles is going to the Lebanon in September.'

Mrs Freeley sucks the tea through her teeth. Delia watches the white sheets she washed early this morning dancing in the wind beyond Mrs Freeley's head. Surreal shapes emerge in the linen as the breeze blows. Beyond, clouds hover in the blue sky.

'I went down to Mikie's and I got a nice rib of beef,' Mrs Freeley is saying. 'He has cut his prices, did you know that? Grand lad, a lot more dacent than the father, tight that fella was, no nature. Mikie is struggling too, no doubt. Did I see Frankie out the back road as I was coming over?'

'I didn't see him.'

Mrs Freeley finishes her biscuit. She takes up the cream handbag she had left on the floor beside her and takes out another More cigarette and her red lighter. She lights up the cigarette, sucking deeply, and then exhales a flowing blue cloud around the front kitchen.

'That was an awful how-do-you-do last night?' Mrs Freeley says.

'What was that?'

'On the television before the news, the quare fellow. How about him practicing what he preaches! I would never have seen it only I put it on for the news and there he was, bold as brass, telling us about the country's problems. I never heard such rawmaish in all me life.'

'Is Lemass going to get back in?' Delia says.

'Oh, you know well, I don't know a lot about it.'

'I mean Fitzgerald, Fitzgerald, I mean.'

Delia collects the cups and puts the brown kettle to boil again.

Thomas arrives on Tuesday. Delia finds him in the front kitchen at half past eight. He kneels in front of the red tiled mantelpiece. His hair dangles from his square skull, rubbing against the brown patterned carpet as he peers under the armchair and the two-seater beside it. He wears braces over a creased white shirt.

'Left something after me the last time,' Thomas mumbles, his face a dark red.

In the back kitchen, Delia ties on her grey faded apron. She pulls out the frying pan from the last press, beside the sink under the cutlery drawer. She opens the fridge door and takes out sausages and rashers.

'You're lucky, I'm just after getting a few messages.'

'Didn't know I was coming until yesterday. Came down with The Patch. We left above at four o'clock, Lord save us!'

'Shush!' Delia says.

Thomas wipes his hands and gets off his knees. He sits at the round table. Delia fries two eggs with the meat in the pan and cuts four slices of soda bread. Thomas eats heartily.

'I'll do a few things while I'm here ma,' he says, as he carves the pink meat from the bacon rind. 'Gone quiet above for a few days.' Thomas places a corner of the yolk on the bacon and places this on top of a small piece of buttered soda bread, before consigning the lot into his mouth.

After breakfast Delia sits in her armchair beside the red tiled mantelpiece. Clouds have taken over the sky. She can see Thomas walk down the path toward the shed where James Meade once fixed bicycles for a living. Thomas tugs at the green door. He shakes the bolt for some moments before sliding it back. He pushes the door in and enters. A small bicycle wheel soars out the door, landing with a clang on the path.

Thomas comes out with two rusty paint cans and some brushes in a cloudy jam jar. He returns inside. He adds a rolling tray and roller to the items on the path. With a screwdriver he prises open the lid of one of the cans and peers in. He pulls a long rusty rod from the grass and stirs the contents.

'I'll paint the box room with this stuff,' Thomas says, as he arrives in the back kitchen with the paint.

'That young laddin' will have no more use for it, I suppose,' Delia says.

Delia hears Thomas padding around upstairs, moving boxes, tearing paper. Sellotape being ripped off the walls sends a sharp noise down the stairs.

'Bleddy posters,' Thomas says. Soon, there is an impatient scraping: scrape-scrape, scrape-scrape-scrape, scrape-scrape, scrape-scrape-scrape, scrape-scrape, scrape-scrape-scrape followed by a bang.

The smell of paint travels down over the brown carpeted stairs and floats along the front hall, through the back kitchen and to Delia, who stares out the tall window. A sponge like noise comes next, accompanied by a gentle thudding and then Thomas whistling.

'Cup of tea?' Delia shouts up the stairs, as the Angelus bell rings on the grey radio she turned on towards midday on the counter in the back kitchen. She lights the gas on the front right-hand hob. The blue flame flickers and she places the half-filled brown kettle over it.

When it boils, Delia pours a small amount of water into the stainless steel teapot on the counter, swirling it around and pouring it down the sink. She puts in three teaspoons of tea leaves from the blue tin tea caddy with Captain Oates on the front and half-fills the teapot with the rest of the boiled water.

Thomas lights a Major cigarette at the round table in the front kitchen. 'Done now,' he says.

'That was quick.'

'I'm a professional, ma,' he says.

'I'm sure,' Delia says.

Thomas brings the paint cans down the stairs. Delia hears sweeping. Thomas washes the brushes, the roller and the tray under the brown brass tap at the shed door. He pours white spirits from a plastic bottle into the jam jar with the brushes and carries everything back into the shed. He comes out holding a rusting hedge clippers.

'You have enough done now,' Delia says, from the back door.

'The day is young yet, ma!' Thomas says, walking down the path.

Thomas starts cutting the hedge which borders the street. At two o'clock Delia begins to stir from left to right in her armchair. She gets up and goes to the tall press, beside the calendar, in the corner of the stump of an old partition between the front and back kitchen which James Meade had removed in 1931 because the family was getting too big to be traipsing in and out of the connecting door. Delia takes out a long handled duster, some yellow cloths and a can of Mr Sheen and goes to the front room.

In the corner of this room, there is a white tiled mantelpiece with an imitation granite top. A small golden clock ticks in the centre. A miniature vase painted with blue decorative designs is at one end. On the other, there is a short red candle on a black steel stand. Above hangs a painting of a mountain.

At the party wall, there is a Challen Evans miniature piano. Its keys are covered with a walnut veneered lid. Across, there is a glass panelled sideboard, on top of which are an empty black fruit bowl, a set of whiskey glasses and a Bible. In the middle of the room, a white doyley is spread across a small coffee table. Three white chairs line the wall bordering the front kitchen.

Delia begins to wipe away the cobwebs from the ceiling. The room becomes hot and she tries to push up the window. She knocks on the glass. 'Thomas! Thomas! Will you open this?'

Thomas is leaning over the hedge with the clippers in mid thrust. Delia hears him swear to himself. Thomas arrives in the front room. 'What are you at, ma? One of the girls will do that, surely.'

'I could be waiting. All this mooching you are doing is giving me notions.'

'Well, that's good, ma.' Thomas' thick arms are exposed, his shirt sleeves rolled up to his biceps. He pushes up the window.

'Fairly stiff. Bit of WD. I'll sort that later,' he says.

Thomas resumes clipping. There is a rhythm to the movement: clip-clip, clip-clip-clip, clip-clip, clip-clip-clip, clip-clip, clip-clip-clip. Delia scrapes away the cobwebs. There is a spider in one. She delicately rolls the duster around the cobweb and the spider. She pulls it down and goes out into the glory hole, into the darkness, to the void. Here, she carefully removes the cobweb from the duster, placing it where she cannot see, and she returns to the front room.

Delia removes all of the items off the top of the white tiled mantelpiece. She takes everything off the sideboard and the coffee table. With a cloth she wipes off the dust from the piano, the coffee table, the top of the sideboard, the mantelpiece. She opens the can of Mr Sheen and sprays all the surfaces. There is a nice fragrance. She shines the furniture with another cloth.

Outside, through the window, Delia can see Thomas struggling to cut a thicker part of the hedge. She hears him cursing the clippers. Thomas leaves them resting on the half-cut hedge and walks around the back. A few moments later, he returns with a small blue can. He sprays the clippers. He resumes clipping. After a few moments he throws the clippers to the ground and walks around the back. He returns with a push along mower and begins cutting the grass in the tiny lawn.

A man walking along the path on the street stops at the black front gate. He wears a pinstripe suit and a trimmed moustache. 'Thomas, is it yourself?'

'Ah, hello Paddy. How are you getting on?'

'Very good, now. Home for a few days?'

'Just a few days. Things are quiet above at the moment.'

'I see.'

'Sure they're quiet everywhere. Them crowd in Leinster House are doing us no favours.'

'Quite, quite.'

'How is the carpet game going?'

'Very well now, very well. I see you're getting ahead with the garden.'

'Well, just doing a few bits for the mother. While I'm here.'

'Great stuff. You won't move back to town, I suppose?'

'No, I'm settled in the Big Smoke. There twenty years now, since I came home from England.'

'Are you indeed. Time flies.'

'Surely.'

'Well, I best keep going, see you again, Thomas.'

'See ya, Paddy.'

'Silver spoon up his arse, that fella,' Thomas says, chewing a piece of soda bread as the six o'clock news comes on after the Angelus on the grey radio on the counter in the back kitchen. 'Never had to kill himself.'

'They do well there. I suppose it takes a bit of managing.' Delia chews part of a jam sandwich. She sits across from Thomas at the round table in the front kitchen.

'Arrah, the father had it set up for him. Did you hear the posh accent of him? And him born here on the Bog Road?'

'Is there not much work in Dublin now, did you say?' Delia says, lifting her cup to her lips.

'There's only bits and pieces, ma. You would want to be moving around the whole time to do anything. It's all over the place that town. You could be travelling the whole day to make a fuckin' pound–'

'Shush, mind your tongue.'

'Well, that's the way it is up there,' Thomas says. He lights a Major and stares out the tall window. Delia takes up the plates and cutlery and washes them at the sink in the corner of the back kitchen.

'Ah, if only I was twenty years younger, I'd make a few quid,' Thomas says.

'How is Barry?' Delia says, as she dries the teaspoons and places them in the cutlery drawer beside the sink.

'Good as far as I know,' Thomas says. 'He did a course, I think. She told me he was going to work abroad.'

'Will he come to visit some day?'

'Arrah, you know she is a bitch, that woman!' Thomas tosses the cigarette into the fire. He gets up, pressing his palms against the top of the round table. It shakes in his wake. 'That fucking woman.' He walks out of the house, banging the front door behind him.

It is late when he returns. The footsteps circle the front kitchen, the doors of the drinks cabinet open over the sideboard at the round table. There is a clink of glasses, a low grunt. A cough. Delia hears him going to the bathroom, running the taps.

Some hours later, she wakes again. Thomas climbs the stairs slowly. She hears his bed creaking in the back room and the crack of a match.

Delia gets up at eight o'clock. She takes her false teeth from the glass of cloudy water on the small table beside the bed, gently shaking them dry and fitting them around her gums. In the back kitchen she ties on her faded grey apron. She pulls out the frying pan from the last press beside the sink under the cutlery drawer. She opens the fridge door and takes out sausages and rashers. She fries two eggs with the meat in the pan and cuts four slices of soda bread. She slices soda bread and arranges it on a side plate. Thomas arrives in the back kitchen. His fingers shake as he takes up the knife and fork.

'I'm going back today,' he says, as he finishes the last sausage. 'A bit of painting has come up. I got word last night in McCambridge's. Can I bring this?' He holds a book by Thackeray. One of the girls bought it at a jumble sale decades ago, it has been under the back room bed since.

Thomas gets the lunchtime train to Dublin. In the evening, Delia feels a draught. The front room window is still open and it is too stiff, she cannot close it. The hedge along the path is half trimmed. One side is a foot higher than the other. Jagged mown sections of the lawn are bordered with tufts of grass. Delia tuts. She shuts the door on the front room to keep out the cold night breeze.

2.

The next day, the sun shines through the tall window onto Delia, who sits at the round table in the front kitchen. Today, there are no sheets on the washing line in the yard, they are neatly folded away in the odd shaped linen press in the front bedroom, above the slanted ceiling over the stairs. Delia sits with her legs crossed underneath the table, awkwardly, as her thighs are wide. In front of her is a sheet of blue lined paper. She writes items on the paper with a ballpoint pen, embellishing every 'r', 't' and 'y'. The sound of her pen movement on the table cuts through the silence of the house on the Bog Road. She writes 'soda bread,' 'eggs,' 'teabags,' 'matches,' 'soap.' She pauses, putting the top of her biro against her lips and writes 'ham' and 'eggs.' She folds the paper into her black handbag. She waddles out to the front hall with her handbag on her shoulder and her blue canvas bag in her right hand. She started waddling after her fifth child.

It is a summery day outside. Delia takes a green wool coat from the coat stand in the front hall and puts it on. On a hook above the mirror hangs a soft black beanie hat which she fits snugly on her head. The air is warm against her lungs. She meets others on the path in the Bog Road. One clutches a similar canvas bag already full of items. One taps a cane walking stick on the concrete. Another tries continually to restore a handbag to a comfortable position on her shoulder. Some smile as they meet Delia, a lone tooth or vacant gums are bared, the lips turn up past the nostril. Their frames soften.

'Morning, Mrs Meade.'

'Morning, Mrs Rafferty.'

'Hello, Mrs Meade!'

'Morning, Mrs Greysforth.'

At the end of the Bog Road, Delia turns right and walks up a hill by a school for children with special needs. A stooped man walks down the hill with the appearance of dragging a weight behind him.

'Hello, Delia.'

'Hello Stephen, how are you?'

'It's a nice day but there is a bit of a chill in it!'

'There is, Stephen. How is your Mother?'

'Oh, grand.'

'Tell her I was asking for her.'

'Oh, I will a course, Delia.'

Along the mall, a figure wavers from left to right. The figure stops, walks, turns around, turns back. Delia checks her pace. Frankie watches lampposts, then people, then scratches his jaw. He wears a dark faded three-piece suit which is several sizes too big for him, the arms of the jacket and the front of the waistcoat are stained with grey and yellow patches.

It takes thirty-five minutes for Delia to get to the post office. As she nears it, she shortens the distance between herself and Frankie. A hip flask appears and Frankie takes a slug before returning it to his left-hand inside pocket. Frankie speaks continuously, not in any intelligible way, a low hum, a mishmash of words. Delia gets close enough that Frankie notices her and he smiles. His eyes open wide and he spreads his arms out as though preparing for a hug.

'Delia!' he says. 'Delia! Will you marry me?'

Two men, in their fifties, stand outside the door of the post office, smoking cigarettes, and spitting on the pavement between outbursts of speech.

'Who knows what this crowd will do next!'

'I don't know what's going to become of this country! Ah, gangsters, gangsters!'

'Gangsters! Hello Delia!'

'Hello Johnny, Peter.'

'Hello, Delia.'

'Grand day.'

'Grand.'

'Fierce gangsters in that Dail.'

'Fierce.'

'Going shopping today, Delia?'

'Well, I'll get a few things in Kevin's.'

'See you again Delia!'

There is a long queue inside. Delia takes the green book of pension cheques out of her black handbag and stands in line. Frankie stays outside. He is quiet now, hands in pockets, peering at three young men inside the door. When one glances out at him, Frankie turns away and walks toward the edge of the path. The young men laugh together.

Delia arrives at the counter. The clerk's skin is smooth, her eyes bright as she smiles. Her auburn hair is neatly trimmed at her shoulders, a fringe curtains her forehead.

'Good morning, Delia.'

'Morning, Paula.'

'How are they all, how is Thomas getting on?'

'Oh, great now. He is still in Dublin.'

'Must be nearly retired now.'

'Soon now I think, Paula. And your girls? Are they in the Sacred Heart?'

'The school? Oh. Oh, no, Mary is in the Council now, Delia. Jeannie is in Dublin.'

'Of course they are. Isn't time flying for us all?'

Delia takes the money off the counter and places it carefully in the green purse which she puts into her black handbag.

Outside, Frankie is singing a song. He pulls a yellow lollipop out of the street bin and sucks it.

'We'll have a white wedding, I think, Delia!' he says.

On the way back Delia stops at Kevin's shop, across from her house on the Bog Road. The shop is busy: pensioners prod fruit and vegetables, squeeze loaves of bread and examine cakes. Delia checks her list and puts the items one by one into her blue canvas bag.

'I was talking to Thomas yesterday, he was in good form,' Kevin says.

'He's just gone back.'

'Ah. I suppose the house will seem empty again.'

'I suppose it will.'

'See you now, Delia.'

'See you, Kevin.'

Delia three-quarter fills the cooking pot with water and submerges the bacon she has taken from the fridge beside the cooker. She puts the pot on the front right-hand hob and sets it simmering. She sits in her armchair beside the red tiled mantelpiece and looks out at the sheets she hung on the washing line early that morning. She watches the surreal shapes which the wind forms beneath the linen. Steam floats around the house. At a quarter to twelve Delia gets up and reaches over to the tall window, beside the round table in the front kitchen and pushes it up a little. The window does not creak and does not need any WD.

The bacon is taken out of the pot at half twelve with a two-pronged fork and Delia sets it on the draining board beside the sink. She puts three medium-sized potatoes in the pot with some cabbage leaves and puts the pot back on the gas.

At one o'clock, Delia drains the pot and puts the cabbage on a plate. She cuts slices off the bacon and sets them beside the cabbage. She peels the three potatoes, tossing them around her fingers at the sink and puts them on the plate. She sits at the round table with a glass of milk and eats. After she has finished, she puts the plate in the sink with the knife and the fork and walks out the back door, taking a brush with hard bristles and sweeping the yard.

There is a knock at the door. Delia waddles through the back kitchen and down the front hall. She pulls back the safety chain and opens the front door. A shaft of light runs across her face. Barbara and her husband Aidan enter. Barbara brings in a carrycot in her left hand. Aidan has a milk bottle in his left hand, the loose hairs of his goatee lift slightly in the breeze which follows them. Behind, holding a train in his right hand, is a brown-haired boy of four years who almost collides with the front door. He rushes through the front hall after his family.

'Mammy, what happened the cooker, did you burn the dinner?' Barbara says as she enters the back kitchen. She goes to the sink and turns on the tap, while Delia sits at the red tiled mantelpiece, looking out the tall window at her sheets on the washing line.

'Do you have any Brillo pads here, mammy?' Barbara says, from within a cloud of steam. The boy plays with the train at the round table. Aidan slouches on the two-seater couch, unfolding the Sunday newspaper and scratching his goatee as he looks at the pages.

The boy wanders off upstairs. In the landing, the door to the box room is open. A speck of yellow paint is on the round black door-knob. Inside, the blankets are neatly tucked on the bed. The walls are bare. The posters have been taken away. Shortly after, he comes down the stairs running.

'Who painted my room?' the boy says.

'Your Uncle Thomas was here, he did a few jobs,' Delia says.

'Oh,' the boy says. 'He painted over my name – that was over the door.' The baby cries.

'With you in a minute, honey,' Barbara says, as she dries the draining board with a cloth.

Barbara takes up the baby from the carrycot. She sits at the round table and, opening her yellow blouse, slides her left nipple into the baby's mouth. The baby sucks hungrily.

'We must put a bed in that other bedroom, so mammy could come out for a night.'

23

'Yes, sure,' Aidan says. He takes out his pipe and lights it. It spreads a faint chestnut smell throughout the front kitchen.

'I was thinking we could put a few plants around the rockery,' Barbara says.

'Yeah. I wouldn't mind a few sycamores as well.'

'They get very big. Shrubs would be better,' Barbara says.

'Hmm. Okay,' Aidan says.

The boy walks around the back kitchen, looking in drawers and presses. He peers into the back of them, moving around plates and bowls as though to get a better view of the darkness. Delia turns her head toward him.

'Keep away from there!' Barbara says. The boy looks at the white door of the glory hole, where Delia had partially completed her rearranging.

'She'll soon be on soft potato,' Barbara is saying.

'Hello, little girlin',' Aidan says to the baby, tickling her chin.

'She got big since she was last here,' Delia says.

'She's a great sleeper.'

'They're opposites so,' Delia says.

'Indeed they are,' Aidan says.

There is a muffled scream. The boy is in the glory hole, the door has closed on him. He cannot get out. He screams, banging, as Aidan gets up and turns the doorknob. The boy's face is deep red as he comes rushing into the back kitchen.

'No child likes the dark,' Delia says.

Delia goes to eight o'clock Mass every weekday morning. During the week, the Bog Road is busy, motor cars speed past. Different people hurry along the path at this time of the day. Some smile and wave as they pass her out.

'Hello, Delia!'

'Morning, Mrs Meade.'

'How are you, Delia?'

The church is a stone cut building across from the mall. Delia arrives twenty-five minutes before eight o'clock.

Inside, there is a smell of brass polish. Footsteps on the vinyl tiles make a soft thudding sound. The choir is empty, there is only a choral accompaniment on Sundays. Along the walls, the Stations of the Cross depict the last hours of Christ. The priest, not yet in his alb, passes through. There are about fifty parishioners in the church, most are over the age of seventy.

Delia takes her usual place. She always sits behind the first of the eight marble pillars at the sixth pew back from the altar, on the outside. James Meade had always sat at the other end, their children between them.

One day in winter, the Meades sat in the front pew. James Meade wore a black tie. A low whining rang around a white coffin that day.

Today she sits alone, part of her grey thinning hair swept back with a brown hairgrip. The priest's housekeeper hurries past the altar.

Delia blesses herself, her wide knees press against the cushioned wood. She takes her rosary beads from her black handbag and begins to slowly feed each bead through her hands. She says a decade of the Rosary while she waits for Mass to begin. The rosary beads are oval, connected by a chain of brass links. One Hail Mary passes through Delia's lips as she grips each bead. Her eyes are directed to the tiles on the floor. She is saying the prayer rhythmically, the words are unintelligible.

The parishioners murmur their prayers, feeding their rosary beads through their fingers. She looks around the church, as though lost. She sits in a summery dress, her hair tied with a red bow and dainty white shoes on her feet in a church with old people at eight o'clock on a Tuesday morning.

Everyone she grew up with is dead.

After Mass, the sun shines in her eyes as she walks down the hill past the school for children with special needs, turning left onto the Bog Road. There is a clipping noise as she nears 109. Mrs Freeley is already in her garden, pruning something in the corner.

'My petunias are getting out of hand, dearie,' Mrs Freeley says from over the wall, as Delia opens her black front gate.

'You have a great selection,' Delia says.

'Trial and error, dearie, trial and error.'

Delia walks inside and puts her handbag on the round table in the front kitchen. She takes off her green wool coat and her soft black beanie cap and hangs them on the coat stand in the front hall. She walks upstairs, takes off her good grey jumper and puts it on the top shelf of the wardrobe. At the bottom, she takes out a green faded cardigan. She wraps it around her, sliding her arms through the sleeves and walks down the stairs, through the front hall and the back kitchen, out through the bathroom and down the path. She arrives at the door of the shed. Thomas has not bolted it and she pushes it in, the door scraping the concrete below.

Here, James Meade stands over his workbench. He pulls a rubber tube from a cardboard box. Before him, beside a worn tyre is a tangled chain, three gear wheels and a can of bicycle oil. A cigarette glows between his teeth as he forces the tube into the tyre, glancing up at Delia, who holds a baby in her arms.

'The dinner is ready, Jimmy.'

'Jesus Christ, woman, I'm flat out, I'll have no bleddy time for dinner today.'

'You were never this busy at Taunton's,' Delia says. In her arms the baby spills a large bubble of sick from his lips.

'Who was it wanted me to lave Taunton's now?'

On Ryan's Road, James Meade steps out the front door at ten minutes to eight, a cigarette in his left hand, a blue canvas bag carrying two pieces of thickly buttered soda bread with slices of butchers' ham in his right hand. Delia kisses him on the lips, his freshly shaved skin smooth against hers. She waves to him as he walks down the path. Thomas clings to her long grey skirt, Anthony is in her arms.

In the evening, James Meade returns with the canvas bag empty on his shoulder, his fingers black from bicycle grease, his shirt loosened, his cap soaked in sweat. A patch of stubble has appeared around his jaw in the course of the day. He walks with one hand stretched deep in his pocket, his shoulders slouched, his face in a half-smile, his eyes glitter through a soft oval.

Delia has the dinner on the square table in the front kitchen of the house in Ryan's Road for James Meade every evening at half past six. Thomas cries some days, about the boys at school, picking on him, he says. Anthony cries all night and most of the day. Delia brought him to Dr Crabbe but it was colic, he said. There was nothing he could give him. James Meade is cross in the morning if he does not get his sleep so he sleeps in the other bedroom for a while.

Delia stands in the doorway of the tool shed. Within, the evidence of Thomas' last visit remains. A paint can is lying sideways on a shelf. Screwdrivers are scattered on the bench. Two clay flowerpots have fallen over and some of the compost has spilt out on the floor. Delia tuts. Thomas was never patient, he could not wait to start school, could not wait to leave school, could not wait to start work, could not wait to stop work. He stands beside Delia now, tugging at her long grey skirt as she tells James Meade that he needs to eat. Thomas is hungry, Anthony wails, no one can hear anything.

The pruning shears is on a low shelf behind a roll of rusting fence wire. Delia takes the shears and walks out into the sunlight and down the path, through the yard, past the scampering black cat, along the gable, pushing from her face the stray strands of the hedge that Thomas half cut. She gets to the tiny garden at the front. Across the wall, Mrs Freeley is examining her roses in a corner. Her garden is bordered with yellow painted brick. Delia begins to trim back the rosebush in the centre of the right-hand lawn. Long strands of rose-less branches stick out across the path, obstructing her passage every day.

'They grow so long and not half enough roses in that type,' Mrs Freeley says.

On Easter Sunday, there is a knock at the door. Delia waddles down the front hall. She pulls back the safety chain and opens the front door. A shaft of light runs across her face. Philly comes in with her husband Jack and their daughter, Rochelle. Philly has a round face. Her straight hair is trimmed at her shoulders. Jack has a comfortable tweed cap on his head. He is over six foot and laughs and snorts at the same time.

'How are you, mammy?',' Hello, Delia,' they say. Philly sits in the armchair where Mrs Freeley usually sits and where Barbara had sat a few days earlier. Jack sits on the two-seater. Rochelle runs around the back kitchen, opening doors of presses and then runs out into the front hall and up the stairs. Delia sits back beside the red tiled mantelpiece.

'Tired after that journey,' Philly says. She stretches back on the armchair. Delia gets up again.

'Were the roads busy?' she says, taking the brown kettle from the cooker, filling it with water and putting it to boil on the front left-hand hob.

'Nothing but buses, wherever they do be going,' Jack snorts. He scratches a large boil on his ankle.

When the kettle boils, Delia pours a small amount of water into the white delph teapot on the counter, swirling it around and pouring it down the sink. She puts two teaspoons of tea leaves into it from the blue tin tea caddy with the picture of Captain Oates on the outside.

She fills the teapot with boiled water. She brings it over to the round table.

Delia takes three cups and saucers from the first press over the counter beside the cooker and brings them over to the round table. The silver sugar bowl is already in the centre.

There is a knock at the door. Delia waddles down the front hall. She pulls back the safety chain and opens the front door. A shaft of light runs across her face. Margaret, smaller than Philly with a sharper chin, and her husband Jack who wears a cream shirt and a blue tie enter, followed by their daughter Michelle. Michelle runs upstairs.

'Hi mammy, Jack,' 'Hello Delia, Philly, Jack,' Margaret and Margaret's Jack say. Margaret's Jack is a little shorter than Philly's Jack and clears his throat before he speaks. He sits beside Philly's Jack on the two-seater.

Margaret takes out the chair at the round table where Delia usually sits eating her dinner and gazing out the tall window, over the yard at the sheets billowing in the wind.

Delia brings over two more cups and saucers and pours the latest arrivals' tea.

'Anything stronger there, Delia?' one of the Jacks says.

'I'll have a look,' Delia says.

Delia opens the drinks cabinet over the sideboard beside the round table and takes out a bottle of Jameson. She takes two glasses from the top shelf and half-fills them with whiskey.

'Anything with it?' Delia says.

'Neat,' Philly's Jack says.

'Drop of water,' Margaret's Jack says.

When they are all seated in the front kitchen, the doorbell rings. Delia waddles down the front hall. She pulls back the safety chain and opens the front door. A shaft of light runs across her face. Mary stands on the path, her curls dangling messily around her shoulders. She holds two shopping bags in her left hand, her daughter Helen's wrist in her right hand.

'Get inside, madam, and not a word out of you for the day.' Mary enters, pulling Helen with her. The child has pushed her lips tightly together and her cheeks are slightly inflated. Her eyebrows dip toward the tip of her nose.

'A few things there for you, mammy,' Mary says, the bags rustling as she passes Delia.

Delia looks out to the street where Mary's two-door car is parked. Within, Mary's husband Jack sits. He stares ahead, tapping the steering wheel with his index finger. When Mary enters the front kitchen, the others look up and the conversation stops. After a moment, Delia walks in by Mary and walks over to her armchair and stands there. The two Jacks stand up.

'Jackie boy with you, Mary?' one of the Jacks says.

'Out in the car,' Mary says.

'We'll move out to t'other room, he'll be in in a minute, will he?' one of the Jacks says. The two Jacks walk out to the front room. Mary sits on the two-seater.

'Cup of tea, Mary?' Delia says and goes into the back kitchen and takes another cup and saucer out of the first press over the counter beside the cooker.

Helen runs in and takes a banana out of one of the bags Mary carried with her.

'Your lady has got big,' Philly says.

'What? It's only a banana?' Mary says.

'No, I mean she's getting tall.'

Delia brings over the extra cup and saucer and places it on the round table. She sits on her armchair beside the red tiled mantelpiece, looking out the tall window at the sheets that she hung early in the morning.

When Mary's Jack enters, he joins the other two Jacks in the front room. They sit at the coffee table on the three white chairs. After a while Mary's Jack goes into the front kitchen and brings the bottle of Jameson out to the front room.

The three girls fight upstairs in the box room. Delia can hear yelling and scratching and biting and screaming. The three of them arrive together in the front kitchen, all pulling at a doll, until one of its arms are torn off. They laugh and whoop, running out to the stairs, leaving the doll on the brown patterned carpet.

The three Jacks' voices drift out of the front room and into the front kitchen where Delia sits.

'Well, how are ye getting on?' Margaret's Jack says, clearing his throat.

'Well, not too bad you know, I hear milk is going down a bit?'

'It's the fecking creamery, sure they are always trying it on,' Philly's Jack snorts.

'You cu'nt be up to them!' Mary's Jack says.

29

'We should have done something about this crowd.'

'We should, we should.'

'Arrah, sure what can you do?' Philly's Jack puts in, to which Mary's Jack agrees, 'Sure what can you do?'

Delia drinks a mouthful of tea and puts the cup down on the saucer on the black hearth and looks around the room. Who are all these people and where is she at all and when is she going to get home? She asks the tall girl with the long blonde hair how she could get home and the tall girl looks at the others and they talk. In the post office, where are her stamps? Someone says does she want to go for a walk on the ferry to England and the sea is rough. She is drinking a cup of tea in her own house in the Bog Road and she is seventy-seven years old.

When Mrs Freeley calls later, saying she would call in, seeing as she heard there were visitors, Delia hears Philly saying to Mary on the qt, 'You would think the old bat would stay at home, can't she see mammy has visitors?'

They leave in stages. They had a big drive and probably wouldn't be home until eleven o'clock and these roads were terrible and Delia was all alone again and she sat at the red tiled mantelpiece looking out the tall window at the stars in the sky.

3.

'That was months ago, dearie. I'll have to get you a calendar. Look, you have one there,' Mrs Freeley is saying. She holds a cup of tea in her left hand and a slice of fruit cake in her right hand. Mrs Freeley bites a piece of the cake. A currant gets stuck between her two remaining front teeth. She licks it away with her long thin tongue. Delia looks directly at Mrs Freeley. 'Was that Charles I saw home last week?'

'It was Delia, and I meant him to call into you, you know, but sure he does be distracted when he is home, what with the golf club and everything. Out to the Lebanon for another six months now, he says. I do be hoping they will leave him in the headquarters, he says he doesn't go on the patrols, but sure you never know, do you?'

'No. Where is Michael now?'

'Still in Johannesburg. Arrah, it's difficult, but he's doing his best, you know yourself. It's not aisy out there, very backward altogether.'

'Another cup?'

'I will dearie, thank you.' Mrs Freeley slugs the remaining tea from her cup. Some tea leaves stick to the short hairs above her lips.

'It was nice to see them all again last week. How are Mary and Jack, after all that old trouble?'

Delia is at the sink filling the brown kettle. She looks at the cream bowl on the draining board. Flakes of corn have gone hard and stuck to the rim. The rest float around in the milk. She puts down the kettle. She strains off the milk down the sink. She tosses the sodden flakes into the green bin she keeps underneath, peeling off the dried in pieces with the edge of a spoon. 'They are getting used to things again.'

'How long was he…away for?'

'Nine months, I think.'

'Well. Let's hope he can stay on the straight and narrow–oooh…' Mrs Freeley puts down her cup on the black hearth and slides her fingers underneath her blue cardigan, rubbing the bones clad with creamy skin.

'Are you alright?' says Delia.

'It's my rheumatism. I'll have to go back to Wilson.'

'Yes. He might give you something.'

'He's not inclined to. He keeps saying "take it easy and see how it goes."'

'Maybe you are better off.'

'Well, I'm not pregnant, so I don't care what he gives me.' Mrs Freeley drinks from her cup. 'You were lucky Barbara turned out alright that time.'

'Yes.'

'She was such a lovely child, so pretty. And full of beans. Like she was in her own little world all the time.'

'Yes.'

'That roof is leaking, mammy,' Margaret says, looking in from the bathroom that James Meade renovated in 1959. She wears a pink shoulder padded blouse over a pencil skirt and a pair of pointed criss-cross ankle strap pumps. Her auburn hair is expanded through blow-drying out around her shoulders. The base of her heels crisply connects with the tiles in the bathroom, a set of black and white vinyl squares a tile merchant once used to pay James Meade when times were hard.

Delia sits in her armchair at the red tiled mantelpiece, slightly angled toward the two-seater where Michelle watches Delia's fingers. Delia demonstrates a complicated manoeuvre with her knitting needle. The child looks across, her eyes widening, as Delia deftly interweaves the wool.

'Now, that's your purl. This will be a lovely cap for winter. And I'll put a nice rose on the side with some blue linen,' Delia is saying. Michelle tries to intervene, her mouth opening and closing, reaching over Delia's hands with her fingers, but Delia gently evades them.

'Let me have a go, granny,' Michelle says.

'In a minute. Just watch how I start you on this line here.'

Margaret's Jack scratches his buttocks through his tight grey trousers as he walks around the back garden. He runs his fingers along his tie. He looks up at the sky, peering for some moments and then looks down again, around the grass and along the hedge.

'He has gotten into some fad for butterflies,' Margaret says, as she looks toward the Belfast sink in the corner.

'Granny, come on!' Michelle says, jumping.

'That sink is worth a few quid, I'd say,' Margaret says.

Delia hands the wool and needles to Michelle and tosses two more briquettes from the stack on the black hearth into the fire. Delia lights a fire every day of the year, regardless of the weather. However, in winter, sprawling flames would shoot up the chimney, tossing sparks onto the hearth, while in the summer, a timid 'v' of two sods smoulders for the day.

'A fire is the heart of a home,' James Meade once said. Delia keeps her fuel in a container in the back yard, walled and roofed with galvanized sheets. A coal man comes every two weeks in the winter from September 1st to April 30th and empties two bags of coal into it. He is a middle-aged man. His face is always black from coal dust. A pen and a little notebook rest in the right breast pocket of his blue overalls. He has a large smile when he meets Delia. The expression takes up most of his face. He likes delivering coal on the Bog Road, he always reminds Delia, because there are none 'of them bleddy steps.'

'These new houses. Up on a fucking mountain, they are half the time!' Delia purses her lips at the expletive and nods as she hands the coal man a roll of twenty-pound notes for the year. He smiles his mouth contortion again, pushing his trolley of coal around the side of the house as Delia stands at the front door, looking at the comings and goings of people on the Bog Road.

'How long is Jimmy gone, now?' the coal man says one day.

'Ten years this year,' Delia says.

'Sound man he was, the poor fella. My father always said he never left a slate long, even in the worst of times.'

'He wouldn't give to say,' Delia says.

'No, not like a lot o' them, the so-called big shots,' the coal man says.

Delia is looking for her wool and needles to show Michelle another technique which would come in handy if she was knitting a jumper or a cardigan. Using a curved needle to introduce a sleeve. Michelle is not sitting on the two-seater. On the table Delia sees the small fruit cake Margaret brought when she arrived and remained there since they left some days earlier.

Delia meets the priest outside the vestry after Mass. He is plump and red-faced. He looks at Delia, his eyes widen as he closes the door. His pupils dart around the area behind Delia, to one side and then to the other. His shoulders tense then soften on his frame.

'Hello, Delia.' His face creases into a warm smile.

'Hello, Father.'

'How are you getting on?'

'Not too bad, Father.'

Delia transfers her weight from one of her brown shoes to the other. The priest turns his body away from Delia, toward the iron gate at the corner of the church car park. 'Father, could I just have a word?'

The priest stops, his mouth opening slightly. 'Yes Delia, what can I do?'

'Well it's, I was wondering if you could help me, I wanted to ask you something, some day, some day you might have some time.'

The priest nods. 'Certainly Delia, do you want to come in for a minute?' He looks at the door of the vestry and takes out a large bunch of keys from his left inside jacket pocket.

They walk into the hall. It leads to a teak door which opens into a small chamber. The room is painted white and noise echoes. The stained-glass windows are plain panels of red, blue and green. There are no images etched on them here. The priest's alb hangs in a full-length oak unit, where there is no door. A silver chalice is stood on a shelf beside the window. On a built-in desk there is a book, open at the centre, with a minute font on wafer thin pages. A sprawling purple cloth bookmark is attached to the spine.

'Take a seat.' They sit on two narrow chairs in front of the desk.

'Thank you, Father.'

'So, how are you, keeping well?'

'Well Father, I'm getting on.'

'Hmm.' The priest nods with a half-smile. 'I am sure you are very young at heart.'

'It's just that, I well...I wondered.'

'Yes?'

'I wondered what I should, I should...'.

'You are wondering what God's plan might be for you now, is that it, Delia?'

'Yes, Father, something...'.

'How many grandchildren do you have now?'

'Eight, Father.'

'And some of them are local?'

'Just Joseph's daughter in the town now. She is grown up...'.

'Yes. And the others?'

'Well, yes there are the three girls in the south and of course Barbara has a young family–'

'Hmm. It seems that you have a lot to be going on with. God wants us to be occupied. Your grandchildren should become your focus nowadays. Now, if you don't mind, I have to start making a few house calls. Is that alright?'

'Thank you, Father.'

Delia walks home from the church, along the mall, through Ryan's Road, past the school for children with special needs. She turns left, up the Bog Road and walks into the front garden of 109 and through the front hall without taking off her green wool coat or her soft black beanie cap. She boils the brown kettle on the front right-hand hob and makes a cup of Bovril and sits beside the red tiled mantelpiece, where there is no fire, only yesterday's ashes, and she looks out the window at the washing line where there are no sheets hanging today and the sky is cloudy.

There are people in the house in the Bog Road again.

'I told you to feed him.' Mary's hair is knotted, she sucks on a cigarette as she looks at Jack with her eyes narrowing at every deep tone in her words.

'No you didn't, woman! Don't be bitching at me!' Mary's Jack tosses the newspaper onto the two-seater and searches for something in his pocket. 'Where the hell are they gone?'

Delia takes the poker from its hook and stokes the fire, a shower of sparks shoot up the joint chimney with 108, where Mrs Freeley lives.

'Every other Sunday you have a great time of it down in the pub while I'm wiping your dog's arse,' Mary says.

'Shush, that language,' Delia says. Mary's Jack opens and shuts his mouth. He lifts one leg, places it back on the floor, then lifts the other, places it back on the floor. He often practices this sequence during his visits to the house on the Bog Road, but usually with less intensity.

'Just be quiet woman, it was you that wanted that fuckin' dog...' he mutters as he walks out the back door. Delia can see his curly black hair moving in the breeze of the afternoon.

'I must have left them here,' Mary's Jack says on his return. He walks around the front kitchen in a circle and out through the back kitchen, into the front hall. His footsteps thud on the stairs.

'You didn't see his reading glasses, mammy?'

'No. Has he reading glasses?'

'He got them a few months ago. He was awful tired all the time and thought he had cancer or something. The doctor in Passage told him to get his eyes tested. It was all the reading that was the problem.'

'I didn't think he was a big reader.'

'It's the racing pages he reads, mammy. All the numbers. He said he lost a lot of money by not getting the numbers right. Wanted to bring the state to court for not picking up on his bad eyesight, you know, when he was being…admitted. But the lads in the bookies told him he'd be wasting his time.'

'Helen!' Mary's Jack shouts, as he returns to the front kitchen, holding out a five pound note. The shout makes his body tremble and the floor vibrates. The glasses in the drinks cabinet over the sideboard beside the round table in the front kitchen clink together. 'Where is she gone?'

'Upstairs playing.'

'Lord Almighty. Never around when you want them.' Mary's Jack sits on the two-seater.

'How is the building going?' Delia asks.

'Not much happening now, Delia. A few small jobs in Passage, that's about it,' he says, peering out the tall window. 'But to get paid from them is the problem.'

'No one pays him, according to himself,' Mary says.

'What does that mean?' Mary's Jack says, staring at Mary. A girl with dark brown hair and a torn yellow cardigan arrives from the front hall. 'Go over to Kevin's and get me twenty Major,' Mary's Jack says.

'I'm hungry, can I get some sweets?'

'I've no money for rubbish. No.'

'We'll have dinner when we get home,' Mary says.

'That's hours away.'

'Go and get me fags, for fuck's sake!'

'I'll put on a few sausages,' Delia says.

'Never mind her, mammy, she's alright.'

'Here, go on! And don't lose me change!'

Delia is alone again. She stares at the novelty cups which her daughter Kathleen had brought home once from Watford. They hang under the shelf over the cooker beside the presses with plates stacked behind the glass doors over the counter in the back kitchen. One cup is shaped like a half-moon and reads 'You asked for half a cup of tea.' Another, a white plastic mug, has a wide crack along the side and the words 'Tea Break' stamped across. Inside there is a clear plastic container so the cup could still be used. Delia looks out again at the blue sky behind puffy clouds. Rays of sunlight stream through the tall window. The dust rises off the brown patterned carpet.

Delia frowns. She hoovered the house earlier. As she looks around, her eyes catch the photograph in the golden frame which hangs near the door to the front hall.

It is of Delia and James Meade standing at the white gate to the back road. Barbara is in Delia's arms. The child looks cross. James is not looking at the camera, he seems interested in something in the other direction, as though he is not aware the photograph is being taken.

Delia is smiling, and James Meade is too, but Barbara is not smiling. Barbara is trying to get out of Delia's strong arms but Delia can hold her easily, for Barbara is only small and Delia is quite big, while the other children behind her are shouting and playing and throwing stones and sticks at each other and James Meade is in a hurry to go back into the house and look for 'the bleddy paper.'

A crow caws as it perches on the apex of the house on the Bog Road. It is autumn. There is a chill in the air. Delia wipes her hand across her yellow apron as she tries to strengthen her grip on the infant.

'Gaaaahh!' Barbara says.

'Shush petting!' Delia says.

'Pa has a right one,' Mrs Freeley says as she watches Pa Geraghty twist a silver wheel on the top of his camera. Pa is a square shouldered man with a loose shirt which is only buttoned partially. His thick fingers seem ill-suited to the delicate levers and dials. However, he conducts each manoeuvre with precision.

Thomas is expressionless at the door smoking a cigarette, looking at the jig acting of Pa. Margaret, Kathleen and Mary run around the yard whooping and shouting as they chase something. Philly trails after them, snots dripping from her nose, her eyes teary, her arms flapping.

'Micksie got it for me in Harlesden, it's a Kodak, a Retina mark two!' Pa Geraghty says. A boy of eight runs around the side of the house and up through the garden past the children. Tears stream down his face, his skin is a dark red.

'Mammy!' the boy says.

'Look at this mannin', well, really, Charles,' Mrs Freeley says. 'Now how did that happen?'

Mrs Freeley puts her arm around the boy's shoulder as she bends down and peers at the red slit across his knee.

'I told you to stop running so fast.'

'There...there was a bucket...in my way...'

A man cycles past on the back road. James Meade watches him, his eyes drifting over the bicycle, the wheels, the chain, the nuts, the threads of the bolts. He misses the work, he tells Delia later, misses the work, misses the life.

Mrs Freeley takes a plaster from her cream handbag and sticks it on the boy's knee. The boy looks at it uncertainly.

'A well you have such a thing in your bag, Agnes,' Delia says.

'You have to carry bandages around when you have little boys, especially like this one,' Mrs Freeley says, rubbing Charles' straight brown hair. Charles runs off down the path, around the four girls playing in the yard.

'You'd want a small hospital with you for our lot,' James Meade says suddenly.

Delia is looking directly at the lens, as Pa Geraghty takes one more photograph, the laughter of her children, the low coughing of Thomas, the occasional murmur of Mrs Freeley come to Delia's ears as she smiles. Delia's eyes are blue, even in the sepia tone of the image on the wall in the front kitchen in the house in the Bog Road, there is something happy about her expression, something content.

It is Saturday night. Delia turns on the tap in the bath. She goes through the back kitchen, through the front hall and up the stairs. In the front bedroom, she takes off all her clothes and takes out a mauve dressing gown from the wardrobe and puts it on. She shakes out her hair and brushes it with a thick red handled brush. She takes off the dressing gown and puts on her underwear, her lace trimmed cotton blouse, her tweed skirt and her light gabardine jacket.

Delia looks in the mirror at the dressing table in the front bedroom and stands back. She sits on the bed. She gets up and stands at the dressing table. She peers closely at the mirror.

Delia walks downstairs and at the coat stand she puts on her soft black beanie hat and her green wool coat. She walks outside into the night, along the Bog Road, turning right up the hill past the school for children with special needs, down through Ryan's Road, where they used to live when Thomas was a small boy and little Anthony was a baby, poor little Anthony. James Meade worked for Mr Taunton when they lived in this house. She slows her pace. Now the house is painted, there are new windows fitted. A small extension has been added to the back. The cinema towers beside it.

Delia crosses the mall and gets to the church. The two big mahogany doors are locked. She turns around and walks down the path.

A black cab drives past. A few youths, some with pink hair, some with shaved skulls, wear blue jeans and denim jackets and stand at the gable of a three-storey block of flats. One sucks on an unfiltered cigarette, the red-hot end glows in the dark, a thick fog of smoke envelopes him. A man walks along, Delia looks directly at him.

'Do you know where Kathleen Johnson lives?' she says. The man does not reply, he does not look at Delia, he is looking at the path as he walks. Delia looks around, her mouth opening and closing.

The finches perched on the chimney pots sing in unison as rays of light break through the grey sky. Delia walks up the Bog Road. Dirty water drifts slowly under the black front gate across the path and down into a drain. She walks through the water, her red slippers soaking it up. The brown patterned carpet in the front hall is covered in a wet film. She walks through, her feet make a squelching sound. A channel runs from the bathroom through the back kitchen. There are shallow pools in the dips of the bathroom floor. The bath is full. Water glides down the side panel. Delia reaches over and turns off the tap.

The next day, Delia is on the front path, sweeping away the dust that had come out the door with the water. She looks at the front door in the cool winter air, at the brass patch form around the keyhole, above at the number 109, underneath the glass panel across the doorway. She walks into the house, wearing new clothes, on a summer's day. The finches sing and the sycamores shake. There are no finches, no sycamores, branches tremble, somewhere in the wind.

Delia feels full. She had been late that month and something was alive again within. The feeling was familiar now. There had been life and death, repeatedly year on year, after Thomas and Anthony, one stillborn in '27, twins in '28. Bridget was born in 1929. She had been a big baby, large blue eyes, crying a lot. Wide fingers for a new-born, James Meade said. Two months later she began to cough and was dead within a few hours. Acute pneumonia, Dr Crabbe said.

Anthony's blue eyes open as Delia enters the back kitchen. His fingers grip the blue wooden bars of the playpen. Curls flop around his jaw. James Meade looks up as Delia comes through the partition door. White sheets of paper are spread out on the round table in the front kitchen. James Meade's stomach heaves in and out as he taps his hand against the corner of the sideboard, a cigarette between his fingers drops blocks of ash on the brown patterned carpet. Delia puts her blue canvas bag beside a vase holding fresh alstroemerias, on the half-moon table, next to the armchair at the fireplace, which was, as of yet, just a hole in the wall. A man from Kilkenny was looking for a cheap fireplace for James Meade.

'Bleddy taxes.' James Meade spits. He gets up from the round table. 'I'll paint the box room.'

The front and back bedrooms he had painted the preceding weeks. They had gotten a deal at the paint shop, six cans of magnolia for three second-hand bicycles.

'Hello there little boy,' Delia says, looking closely at Anthony in the back kitchen.

Anthony smiles, his lips curling up past the nostrils on his minute face. 'Ma! Wan out! Wan out!'

'You want to get out, do you?'

'Wan out! Wan out!'

Delia lifts the boy out of the playpen and puts him on the floor, where he runs off toward the white door of the glory hole.

'In dere? In dere?' Anthony says.

'Nothing in there, ladding!'

'Noging?'

'Nothing.'

'Monkers?'

'Monsters, yes. Keep away from there.'

'Monkers, in dere?'

'Yes.'

Anthony nods and walks around the back kitchen. He opens a press door under the counter. The cooking pot falls out on his toes. He cries.

'I told you not to be jig-acting, Anthony,' Delia says, picking him up, rubbing his toe and placing him in the playpen again.

'No, no paypin, no.'

Delia walks in from the front garden, out of the light and into the empty house.

In a pound shop at the end of Main Street, Delia finds two aisles of cheap toys: cowboy pistols, modern dolls, hula hoops, bicycle horns, boxing gloves. She chooses a train for the boy and a thin yellow haired doll for the girl. The shop does not have any Christmas wrapping paper.

'None at the moment, ma'am,' the teenage girl says, fiddling with one of her earrings. Delia finds a roll of wrapping paper in the wardrobe in the front bedroom. It is decorated with the repeated image of Santa Claus riding a sleigh pulled by reindeers through the sky. In a drawer of the sideboard underneath the drinks cabinet in the front kitchen, below her knitting set, Delia finds some red ribbon and takes out a large orange handled scissors. She ties each parcel with a neat bow.

'Why have you dressed them in such light clothes? Look at that lady and not a stitch on her,' Delia says when they arrive, the boy, now six, standing beside her, the girl now three, pulling at Delia's green cardigan sleeve. The boy sucks an ice lolly, his eyes stare at Delia. Aidan sits on the two-seater, reading the Sunday newspaper. Barbara is washing three plates in the sink. She scrapes the crusted remnants of bacon off them with a steel wire scourer.

Barbara's children take the presents, the boy muttering 'thanks,' and they open the wrapping paper and run off. Delia is suddenly tired and sits back in her armchair at the red tiled mantelpiece.

Delia looks at the calendar hanging beside the tall press between the back kitchen and the front kitchen. From her armchair to the wall she cannot discern the numbers or the four red letters of the month. All she can make out is the picture, a clear view of a mountain with a green forest in the foreground.

Delia looks around, there is no one at the sink, the noise of the children playing upstairs has stopped, she can only hear a distant car exhaust. She sits back again and looks out the tall window at this morning's sheets billowing in the wind. Within the red tiled mantelpiece, the fire smoulders. The flames have died away. She sighs.

Delia sits alone at the round table in the front kitchen, making a list with her ballpoint pen. She lists out names: Thomas, Anthony R.I.P., Michael R.I.P., Frances R.I.P. and Francis R.I.P., Bridget R.I.P., Joseph, Donal R.I.P., Sam ?, Molly R.I.P., Margaret, Kathleen, Mary, Philomena, Barbara. Delia looks at the names, her eyes reading, her head nodding, the names on the blue paper become faces, faces of people, faces of lives. They laugh and play, run and jump, pull at her faded grey apron, toss their hair, squeal and cry, wail and roar.

Delia writes down more names: Kathleen R.I.P., Maisie R.I.P., Maud O'Grady (nee Hopkins) R.I.P., Tom O'Grady R.I.P. Delia looks out the window at the sheets blowing in the breeze.

Barbara says, 'You are putting the wrong names on faces, mammy, that's all.'

'Everyone forgets a few things when they get a bit older,' Aidan was saying. The boy keeps beating a drum, making a bum-bum, bum-bum-bum sound, more like a slap, then a real drum noise.

'Stop it,' Barbara says.

'Go out and play, good lad,' Aidan says.

When Delia gets back to the house on the Bog Road, Mrs Freeley is turning off the tap at the kitchen sink.

'Left on the tap, dearie,' Mrs Freeley says. Delia tapes a note over the sink to remind her to turn off the tap, but she does not always look at the note when she finishes washing her plate and cup and knife and fork. She still sometimes puts everything away and leaves the tap running. She had always done the washing-up with the tap running.

Mrs Freeley is talking, holding a burning More in her left hand. Delia drinks from her cup, her eyes drifting over the top of the red tiled mantelpiece in the front kitchen, the golden clock in the middle Kathleen once brought home from Watford which ticks in the silence between Mrs Freeley's outbursts of speech, a plastic statue of St Martin, tiny animals lie beside him on his pedestal, a framed postcard from Australia which Sam sent in the 1950s, a miniature red vase that Megan, her cousin in Boston brought home once, an unlit Advent candle at the other end. Delia looks out the tall window at the surreal shapes forming in the white sheets from the evening breeze and the puffy clouds behind, mooching along in front of the blue sky, the pure, clear sky.

Delia climbs the rickety old ladder that James Meade made many years ago and Thomas had refurbished with some white deal offcuts. Above her head are two glossed pieces of plywood against which she pushes, her fingernails clacking on the smooth finish. The boards slide back and Delia reaches in, pressing the light switch. Dust swirls as bands of shadows border the bright. She emerges in the space above, the air colder here, a breeze around the roof outside transmitting a dull shudder through the slates.

There is a musty smell. Dusty jacketless books are piled up against the chimney breast. Delia steps onto the floorboards Thomas nailed down. They creak as she transfers her weight from the ladder to the ceiling joists.

Delia steps slowly around the attic, looking at a sheepskin jacket, a tweed peaked cap, a pair of bellbottomed jeans, some flannel trousers and a stack of patterned shirts amongst the ageing cardboard boxes. She runs items from a blue cloth bag through her hands: a large white necklace, one green earring, a snow globe of London.

A collapsed shoebox of photographs lies lidless at the end of the floored area between the ceiling joists. The pictures have slid out on the shrunken fibreglass. Philly in her communion dress, in the centre of Mary, Margaret and Kathleen. A wedding group picture, Delia and James Meade at one end. Molly holding her schoolbag, standing at the black front gate of the house on the Bog Road.

Some are not staged. A photograph taken from the stairs as three men walk towards the front door. Sam, Donie and Joseph dressed in white shirts and straight black trousers, hair sleeked back. In another, Frankie, aged about 15, holds a flag in the air, staring intently at the street behind the camera. The movement of Delia's grey eyes slows as she peers at the others. Barbara at a shop counter, Kevin hands her an ice cream. Two girls of about ten years deep in conversation, she does not recognise them, but guesses they are from the Bog Road.

There is a scene in a pub, a trio with arms around shoulders. Two of the men she meets every week at the post office. Here, they are much younger, caught in a burst of laughter. Thomas stands in the centre with a half-smile, a cigarette dangles between his lips. There is one small sepia toned photo of Sam aged about 10 in the back garden, his wavy blonde hair covers his ears, his face is turned to the side, looking up, at the sky. Delia wonders about his thoughts when the photograph was taken. She wonders if he is alive or dead.

Through the tall window in the front kitchen, Delia sees the black cat is back in the yard, prowling around. Delia takes out the carton of milk from the humming fridge and fills a saucer. The black cat arrives at different times. Some months before she left out a saucer when he was not there and other cats came and drank the milk. Now she only puts out the saucer of milk when he is in the yard.

The cat looks up suddenly when he hears the door open and hurries over to Delia. The back road is quiet, only rarely does a vehicle pass. Local farmers had once used it for moving cattle around the outskirts of the town. Delia leaves the saucer down for the cat and he sips. The cat's fur is sleek and he purrs as Delia rubs his back gently.

4.

A man calls one day. 'To read the meter, ma'am,' he says. The meter man has a small step ladder with him, which he unfolds and places on the patch of linoleum around the front door.

'That's not a local accent. Where are you from?' Delia says.

'Meath, originally,' the meter man says. 'I married a local woman.'

'Will you have a cup?'

'Well, I don't usually take anything, I bring a flask with me, ma'am. But I suppose it is eleven, so I might, if it is not too much trouble.'

'No trouble at all,' Delia says.

After he had read the meter, the meter man follows her into the front kitchen. She has set the stainless steel teapot and a plate of arrowroot biscuits on the round table. The meter man sits on James Meade's chair.

'Really, tea was fine, ma'am. Mind if I smoke?' the meter man says.

'No, work away.'

'This is very kind of you, ma'am. Indeed I hardly ever get offered anything.'

'Really?'

'Oh. You would be surprised at people. Very surprised.'

The meter man says something to her father that she does not understand, something about politics. He will take the horses her father wanted to sell, had to sell. The man is a bastard, her father says, when the man is gone.

'Don't be saying that a front a the child,' Delia's mother says, kneading a big lump of dough at the kitchen table. Delia goes up to her room to show her mother one of her dolls but cannot find it and when she comes down her mother is gone. Her father is gone too. Delia does not know why the front door is open and who was drinking from the half-empty bottle of Jameson on the round table.

Delia sits at the red tiled mantelpiece in the front kitchen in the house in the Bog Road, looking out through the tall window across the yard at the sheets lifting in the wind and a piece of coal falls out onto the black hearth and bounces, landing on the brown patterned carpet. A flame rises into the air, smoke billows toward the ceiling. Delia can only see the sheets in the yard through a grey cloud. She coughs, there is smoke going down her throat. The fumes are thick and heavy.

There is a small circle of fire on the brown patterned carpet. She gets up and fills the brown kettle with water and pours it over the flames. 'The carpet was damp,' Mrs Freeley says. She taps her shoe on the charred patch. She sits back in the armchair across from Delia.

'Just as well, otherwise the house would a gone up and mine along with it.' Mrs Freeley's eyes flicker at Delia, more than usual.

Dr Crabbe had long since died and there is a young G.P. practicing locally, a Dr Wilson. His surgery is out the Coast Road, past the school for children with special needs. It takes Delia twenty minutes to walk there. The secretary writes out a time and date on a card. 'I'm forgetting things, dearie, could I see him today?'

'You'll have to wait then.'

Delia sits in the white room watching a boy play with Lego. Music blares from a radio in a corner. A girl of early twenties sits across from Delia. The girl's fingers are intertwined on her lap. There are dark purple stains around the girl's eyes.

Delia's many children run around the waiting room, fighting over cloth toys, which leak foam. One of the girls bangs on the windows. 'Leave the window alone, Philomena!' Delia says.

Delia enters the examination room. Dr Wilson is a fresh-faced man of about thirty. He smiles and shakes Delia's hand. 'How's the family? Thomas still keeping well in Dublin?'

Dr Wilson attaches a red plastic pad to Delia's arm and inflates it. He places the diaphragm of his stethoscope on her chest. He looks in her ears and her eyes with a light.

Dr Wilson writes 'good' in the physical health box on a piece of card. 'What seems to be the problem?'

'Well,' Delia says. 'Doctor, I'm forgetting things.'

'What type of things, Delia?

'Ahem...'. Delia tightens her grip on her black handbag. 'The...there was a bit of a fire in the house last week, the carpet...'.

'I see.'

Dr Wilson writes something on a yellow piece of paper. 'I'll give you these, they are called Benzoctamine, they should help. Come back in two weeks.'

'Thank you Doctor.'

Delia goes to the chemist on Main Street with the yellow piece of paper. A smiling girl hands Delia a small package.

At night, Delia takes a pink pill from the package and swallows it with a drink of water.

Next morning, Delia takes up the green alarm clock on the small table beside the bed and winds it thirty-two times.

In the front kitchen she sets out a plate and a knife and a fork and takes rashers and sausages from the fridge and fries one egg with the meat in the frying pan from the first press under the counter beside the cooker on the front left-hand hob.

Delia butters four slices of soda bread and makes a pot of tea in the stainless steel teapot and shouts 'Thomas!'

Delia looks at the clock with the Roman numerals on the wall beside the golden framed photograph in the front kitchen. It is half past four.

'I hope the schoolbooks will be the same in fourth class,' Delia says. Philly will not answer her.

'When will Thomas be home, Jimmy?' she asks, looking at the Bush television beside the tall press in front of the calendar. 'I hope he goes aisy on the porter, this time.'

James Meade does not answer her.

Delia is walking in her feet, through grass, the sun shines on her cheeks, the stone grey clouds drift like ribbony cotton strolling across the sky. Her feet are tickled by the glass blades around her toes. Flushed children grip the edges of small wooden boats which swing six feet off the ground. The children laugh and scream as they are thrust through the air. A toddler runs along the dusty ground, licking an ice cream. Teenage girls chatter and walk quickly past Delia. Two men stand at the rope and stakes which outline the border of the carnival, their shoulders slouched, their arms swinging aimlessly.

Delia looks across the field at a handsome man in his twenties, standing beside a smaller man. The handsome man has a strong jawline, a squarish head, a flat stomach and broad shoulders. His white shirt is tight around his upper torso, his breeches hold up grey trousers above brown boots with yellow laces.

The handsome man playfully punches the shoulder of his companion and laughs, his head tossing back a thin strand of sandy hair, it swings in the air, around his crown. A dot of white flashes in each pupil of his eyes, where the light reflects.

There is something about the handsome man's jawline, his bone structure that is somehow different from other men at the carnival this day, somehow elegant.

Maisie follows Delia's gaze and jabs at her ribs lightly and they both laugh. Maisie pulls Delia by the elbow. Delia's breath shortens a little, she feels excited.

The smaller man sucks on a cigarette and looks toward Delia and Maisie. He says something to the handsome man. Delia and Maisie reach the two men. Someone makes a remark and Maisie makes a remark and somehow they are all talking and now Delia is talking a little to the handsome man, his name is James.

5.

Delia has lost her shoe. She searches in the front kitchen, at the two-seater, under her armchair, behind Mrs Freeley's armchair, at the back of the sideboard, around the feet of the round table.

Delia walks into the back kitchen, opening the presses over and under the counter. She goes into the bathroom, checks behind the sink pedestal, around the toilet bowl, at the back of the bath panel. There is no shoe here.

Delia goes into the front hall, looking under the flat panel at the bottom of the coat stand. She goes into the back kitchen and opens the door into the glory hole and peers into the darkness. The cloth chest is closed. The photographs lie on the lid, the cutting of Mr Flounders on top. The line of jackets leads toward the void. Her shoe is not here.

Delia looks in the front room, around the piano and under the coffee table, in the sideboard. There is no shoe here. Upstairs, she looks around the box room, under the bed, around the boxes of children's books and toys. Delia sees a little monkey, with one of his glass eyes missing. Her shoe is not here.

 Delia checks the back room, around the double bed, looks in the tall shiny teak wardrobe, underneath it, behind the bedside locker. In the front bedroom, she peers into the odd shaped linen press above the stairs.

At the bottom, below the shelves of sheets and blankets, there is an assortment of footwear. There is a pair of modcloth suave saunter heels which Megan had brought home from Boston. Underneath are Molly's Walkey clogs and a lone leather Loake brogue. Delia's shoe is not here. She looks in her wardrobe, lifts folded clothes, her breath shortening, her eyes watering. The shoe is not here.

Outside, she walks around the garden, peering under the rose-bushes, behind the privet. She walks along the Bog Road, asking passers-by, 'Have you seen a shoe?'

'A shoe, Delia? Haven't seen one, must be getting along now.'

Delia goes into Kevin's.

'Hello, Delia, how are you today? We have some lovely apple tarts from the bakery in–'

'Did you see my shoe, Kevin?'

'Your shoe? No. Do you know, I didn't. Ahem–'

While Kevin is still talking, Delia walks off, out of the shop, across the road, cars brake suddenly. She walks into the house and up the stairs and stands in the front bedroom and sees her two brown shoes behind the hanging end of the blanket under the bed. She looks down at the soft red slippers on her feet.

Delia sits on the bed, looking at the slippers. There is grime on the base of them. They are worn from rubbing against the edge of the black hearth over the years. They were a present that Molly gave her one Christmas.

The soles of them are thin and water has seeped in from the street. Delia takes the brown shoes over to the odd shaped linen press. She places them inside, near the doors, in front of a folded pile of nappies.

'Tell him you're a man with a family, Jim,' Delia says, pinning the cloth around Bridget's waist. James Meade taps his pipe against the end of the sideboard. Delia goes over to the round table and takes away James Meade's plate.

'The amount of people who go to him with their bicycles. You're more or less running that shop.'

James Meade goes to work. Mr Taunton's shop stands apart from a line of terraced houses on Linen Street. Instead of going over to his work bench and taking up his tools as usual, James Meade takes off his cap.

Another consignment of bicycles had arrived from Dublin and Larry, the other mechanic, places them near the front window for customers. Mr Taunton points out the positions he wants and walks to the back of his shop and into his office. Twisting his cap in his hands, James Meade walks down the shop to the office.

Through the glass panel, James Meade can see Mr Taunton writing something in a large black book. Mr Taunton's eyebrows create a disconnected 'V' which is more noticeable when he looks up as James Meade knocks and opens the door.

'Eh, Mr Taunton, can I have a word?'

'Come in, Jim.'

James Meade enters the office, still twisting his cap. The desk is covered in papers: invoices, letters, bills, order sheets. 'It's...I was wondering. Well. I'm tight enough in the wages...'

'It's hard times for us all Jim. Don't worry, I'll look after you, Come here...' Mr Taunton's tone becomes light. He opens a drawer under the desk. He pokes around for a few moments. James Meade leans forward.

'Here is the list,' Mr Taunton says. 'First a few things wrong with Mrs Armstrong's High Nelly. Good man.' James Meade takes the sheet of paper. Mr Taunton writes in his large black book.

James Meade carefully closes the door of the office behind him. Larry looks up from the display at the front as James Meade walks toward his work bench against which several bicycles rest.

'In bother, Jim?' Larry says.

'Ah, I wanted a day off in a few weeks.'

'And did you get it?'

'He said he'd see.'

On Friday, Mr Taunton gives James Meade a loaf of bread. 'Just something for the family, Jim.'

'Thank you, Mr Taunton, thank you very much.'

'Go aisy, Jim, you have a lot on your plate.' But James Meade did not hear him. He was out the door with the bread.

James Meade hands in his notice of resignation to Taunton. He walks out of the shop, feeling like a free man. With the help of Frank Moran, a young labourer from Number 84, he builds a shed at the back of the garden using money he had put away during his years with Mr Taunton. He puts in a few shelves, a work bench and buys a lot of tools.

When people get to know about Meade's new garage in the Bog Road, they stop going to Mr Taunton's shop and Mr Taunton eventually closes the shop down because he couldn't do the work anymore without James Meade, so it is said.

James Meade is making twice the money for half the work and he has a happy wife and three sons and another child on the way. Things could not get any better. James Meade is so busy now that he has people coming from all over town, customers with punctures, faulty brakes, loose saddles, warped mudguards. When he starts fixing bicycle lights, people find out he is great at this 'wiring crack' as well and get him to fix all sorts of electrical problems in the houses in the Bog Road. James Meade is making a ton of money and he buys a few nice things for the house, a Grunow radio set, a fancy half-moon table for the front kitchen and a second-hand piano, a Challen Evans Miniature, which he thinks Thomas might learn.

Anthony is up early. Delia is asleep in the front bedroom. James Meade sits on the edge of the mattress, smoking a cigarette. Anthony walks down the stairs in his pyjamas and walks out the front door. It had been left off the latch from the night before when James Meade had been talking to a customer at ten o'clock. Anthony sees a steam-roller on the road. Men from the council were tarring the Bog Road. It had not been done very well during the original construction. There had been no right boss over the job on the Bog Road after Flounders had done himself in. Anthony sits on the edge of the path watching the wheels of the steam roller press down the tar smoothly. The heated bitumen releases clouds into the low morning temperature.

Anthony begins to shake. He does not notice, he is absorbed in the movements of the machines, the flattening of the soft steaming substance underneath.

James Meade comes down and finds Anthony coughing on the path. He brings the boy inside and wraps a blanket around him. Anthony's skin is bright blue. Thomas is sent to call Dr Crabbe. They give Anthony Bovril, but he does not warm up. Dr Crabbe comes. He tells them that Anthony has Hypothermia. They put Anthony to bed in the box room. The next day, Anthony would not wake up. He lay still in the bed, like a statue. Joe Freeley calls Dr Crabbe. Dr Crabbe comes and checks Anthony. He tells Delia that her son is dead.

6.

At the tall window, Frankie peers into the front kitchen. His nose is long in between two wide oval eyes, bloodshot around the light blue. His grey hair is cropped against his lined neck. His breath blows against the glass. His complexion is dulled through the mistiness of the window. Delia has woken in her armchair. Frankie stares at her. 'Go home, Frankie, what are you doing there?' she says.

'Marry me, Delia,' Frankie says, his face breaking into a smile. 'Ahhhh,' he moans.

'Go on, Frankie, go home,' Delia says. Frankie stays at the tall window for a long time, staring at Delia. His wide smile fades. He becomes expressionless. His diamond-shaped head blocks out the light and greys as his nose presses against the window.

'Go home,' Delia says again. She looks out at the sheets on the washing line. They hang still. There is no breeze today. When she looks back at Frankie, he has gone.

Thomas is saying 'What are you talking about, ma, Jaysus, you must be on the wrong bleddy tablets. Bleddy doctors!' Thomas carries his worn blue suitcase upstairs.

Later, Delia hears an electric razor and smells a nice aftershave. She puts three eggs in a saucepan and puts them into the fridge and sits on her armchair beside the red tiled mantelpiece. Thomas, now cleanshaven, comes into the back kitchen. He looks around the cooker and swears and looks in the presses under the counter and opens the door of the fridge which hums beside the cooker and takes out the saucepan of eggs and he says, 'You're ravelling, Ma!'

Thomas eats heartily. He grunts as he swallows each mouthful. He licks his lips as he clears his plate and takes out a Major from the green box on the round table. 'Ah, it's gone to hell in Dublin, the carry-on of them…fierce men…pay ya? Pay ya? Not at all!…only when it suits them…gangers…using a crane wan day and a fella came with a little book and started taking all our names…there was a buck…Pakistan…ha, ha!...' Thomas is laughing as he smacks the top of the table. 'Ah fierce men, fierce men!'

Thomas touches the cigarette against the edge of the ashtray, slowly tapping the beige butt with his index finger. He burps and stretches back in the chair. He goes upstairs while Delia washes their two plates. She hears him humming. He comes down wearing a tie.

'I'll see you later, Ma,' Thomas says, putting on his suit jacket.

'Is it five, yet?' Delia says. She sits at the round table eating a slice of soda bread. Her tea steams in front of the tall window as she looks out into the yard.

'Around that, I suppose.'

'Well, you're going early.'

'I'll be back around eight, want to see a few of the lads.'

When Thomas is gone, Delia turns on the grey radio on the counter in the back kitchen. A play is on. A woman laments the loss of her son at sea. She wonders how she can kill herself. There is music and a conversation with her dead son, whose voice sounds like it is in a bathroom. The play fades from Delia's consciousness quickly and she falls asleep on the armchair at the red tiled mantlepiece, the light from outside fades until only embers glow in the darkness.

Thomas returns at one o'clock. He sings. 'Fifteen men on a dead man's chest! Yo-ho-ho and a bottle of rum! Drink and the devil did it for the rest! Yo-ho-ho and a bottle of rum!' His voice travels up the stairs to the front bedroom where Delia lies awake. The door is ajar, she sees Thomas pass on his way to the back room. His tie is gone and his shirt is opened. He has a bottle of Harp in his left hand. He speaks for almost an hour in the back room.

Delia fries one egg in the frying pan. Thomas rubs his forehead as he stands in the bathroom. His cigarette unfurls a long thin line of smoke, rising up to the ceiling and out through a pinhole of daylight at the top of the wall, around which there is a dark green patch.

'The fella that put that roof on for himself was a bollocks, do you know that, ma, do you? If I ever meet him, I'll give him a good kicking,' Thomas says.

'Shush!' Delia says, sitting in her armchair beside the red tiled mantelpiece. At half past ten, Thomas walks across the street to Kevin's and comes back with *The Racing Post*. He sits on the two-seater. He gets up, putting on his suit jacket, now creased. He slips back on his brown boots.

'I'm going to Long Street. Back in half an hour.'

Thomas returns an hour later. He adjusts the dial on the grey radio on the counter in the back kitchen. He sits on the two-seater. He holds some yellow slips in his left hand. *The Racing Post* is open beside him. He has taken off his brown boots, their yellow laces dangle across the brown patterned carpet. He taps his stockinged feet beside the boots. His teeth are bared. 'When are they going to put on the twelve fifteen, for bleddy hell's sake,' Thomas says.

'Shush, that language!' Delia says. The commentator speaks in an excited voice, which intensifies as the race progresses. Thomas leans forward on the two-seater, as though to get a better view, his shoulders moving in time to the commentator's voice. The voice gets louder.

'Go on!' Thomas says.

When the race is over, Thomas sits back staring out the tall window. At one o'clock, Delia gets up and puts the brown kettle on the front right-hand gas hob.

'Do you want a sandwich?'

'No,' Thomas says.

Thomas had closed the window in the front room on his last visit and Delia is cleaning the window board where dust and leaves had blown in. A Mercedes drives along the Bog Road and comes to a stop outside Mrs Freeley's house.

Delia watches Charles Freeley slowly get out of the Mercedes. He is dressed in a light green uniform with small coloured badges on the left breast. The jacket has brass buttons and the trouser is creased. There is a dark green stripe running along the leg. His brown leather shoes shine in the sun. Mrs Freeley walks out the path to the white front gate, where Charles, cleanshaven, kisses his mother on her soft wrinkled cheek.

'Mother,' Delia hears Charles say.

'Went for a round of golf then,' Mrs Freeley tells Delia a few days later, when the Mercedes is gone. 'Had a drink with the boys at the club. He meant to call in to you to say hello, but there wasn't time.'

'Kevin told me you were leaving the front door open when you go to the post office, Mammy,' Barbara says. Mrs Freeley is gone. 'It is a bit dangerous. Someone could come in and steal things.'

'Not much for them to steal here,' Delia says.

'Still. Do you want to come out to the Country for a couple of days, at all?'

'No, I'm fine here.'

Delia shivers in her armchair, beside the red tiled mantelpiece in the front kitchen of the house in the Bog Road, alone she sits. She sighs and looks out the tall window, over the yard, white sheets billowing in the wind, surreal shapes forming under the linen, and behind, a cluster of clouds slowly spreads out across another fine blue sky. It rains heavily against the tall window, the sheets get wet, dark spots of water appear all over them. It is sunny, there has been no rain for months. It is too wet to have linen out there on the washing line. Delia does not move.

The house is empty. The house is full. Many people walk through the empty house in the Bog Road. Delia sees them all as she sits beside the red tiled mantelpiece. Delia sees no one. Delia looks around at the front kitchen and the back kitchen and the door to the bathroom and the door to the front hall and the door to the glory hole. Delia sits back in her armchair. She is content.

'Are you moving out to the Country?' Mrs Freeley says.

'What's that?'

'Barbara said to me yesterday you were thinking of moving out to the Country.'

'I don't know.'

'Well, you would have plenty of company,' Mrs Freeley says. 'But then again it would be a big change. How long are we here, now Delia? Forty, no fifty years?'

'Yes.'

'Do you remember when we all moved in? The draw for the houses?'

'I do.'

'The councillor, like he was the Taoiseach, in the middle of the road out there, giving us our tickets. Putting us in our place. Ah well. He's long dead now. When did ye buy yere's out, a few years after, when Jimmy had the garage, was it?

'Around then, I think.'

'Yes. We didn't buy ours out until after the carry-on, when the rations stopped. Just as well we did. I wouldn't like to be still paying rent, the Lord knows what it would be by now. It was dear enough at the time. We were dilly-dallying. Sure Joe was always holding off.'

'There's no point rushing anything.'

'Lord save us, that man never rushed anything, and that's for sure. Jimmy was a great man to do things, he had great go in him.'

'It didn't always work for him.'

'No. Well, you can't blame a man for trying, Delia. He was unlucky with a few things, that was all. Well, I suppose you'll want to think about it for a while.'

'Yes.'

The sun is shining. Delia can hear the beat of a drum. Children shout and laugh, waving their arms, wearing Sunday clothes, boys in neat shirts and short linen trousers, girls in flowing flowery dresses, sandals, ribbons in their hair. In the corner of the field, there is a tall wooden pole with streaming bands of different colours attached to the top. Some children run around the pole, holding the ribbons, the colours merge together as the children run faster. One small boy falls and bursts into tears, snots fall from his nose.

It fades. It is gone. Delia is alone. There is no noise in the house in the Bog Road. The sheets on the washing line hang still. Delia looks at the clock with the Roman numerals on the wall behind the two-seater. It is ten minutes to noon. The second-hand ticks around the face. The clock is battery powered.

There is no need to wind it every second day, like the green alarm clock on the small table in the front bedroom. The battery must be changed every seven years. Delia does not know when she last changed the battery in the clock.

Delia gets up off the armchair. Reaching across the two-seater, she takes the clock down. It is square-faced, black and gold with a long decorative point at the bottom. There is another moulded peak on the top. At the back, there is a small mechanism which powers the clock. The square face indicates a large contraption, but at the back, it is revealed to be merely the size of a matchbox, with a square battery attached underneath. There are specks of corrosion around the terminals. Soon the clock will stop because the battery will be expended.

Delia sits in her armchair. The sides have become smooth from her arms rubbing on them for many years. Her slippers are worn. The red mat beneath her feet is turned at the corner from being slid up against the black hearth for so long. Everything is old in the Bog Road. Everything will be new in the Country. Delia is old. The Bog Road is old. The country house is new. She does not know anybody in the Country.

Delia is lost in a black space. Stars and planets and airlessness. She sits in her armchair, the house is gone, she is alone, outside the Bog Road. She does not know where she is going. There is nobody coming in the opposite direction. Events, events. People. Places and then.

Lost in the space outside the Bog Road. And where? Terror creeps through. Terror and fear. No breath. No breath. No way. No way.

A large black being begins to grow in the corner of the front kitchen, swallowing the round table, the drinks cabinet, the sideboard, the tall window, darkening the room. Delia cannot see. She can see the black devouring the front hall and the front room, the round table from the front kitchen is on the stairs, as though trying to climb the stairs to escape the black, but it cannot.

Delia sits in her armchair in the front room and feels around her calf, down to her ankle and around her red slipper and the brown patterned carpet underneath.

Days go by fast. Morning, afternoon and evening. Sunrise to sunset. Sheets and breakfasts and teas and dinners and visitors and comings and goings and goings and comings and comings and goings and goings and comings.

'This has been an awful winter,' Mrs Freeley says, sucking on a More.

'Terrible,' Delia says, drinking her tea. 'But the spring is here now and the days are getting a bit longer.'

'Yes, indeed, dearie. I like February.'

'It was my mother's birthday yesterday,' Delia says.

'Ah yes, I remember you saying that this time last year. She would be a fair age now if she was still in it.'

'A hundred and ten!' Delia says and they laugh. Delia's eyes glint in the evening light.

'Have you all your presents got for Christmas?' Delia says.

Mrs Freeley does not answer. She sucks again on her More cigarette and Delia looks at Mrs Freeley's yellow fingers holding the brown stem tightly,

James Meade was very distracted after they buried Anthony. He went to the grave every morning. They had bought a plot at a corner of the graveyard on the Coast Road. At the top of the grave, they erected a grey stone with two angels carved on the top right-hand corner and the words 'Anthony Benedict Meade 1926-1931' inscribed.

James Meade did not open the shed in the back garden of the house in the Bog Road until after ten o'clock anymore. People would be queuing up in the back road waiting for him. Young men, old men, tall men, short men, fat men, thin men, men well-dressed in long jackets, men in dirty torn shirts, some in duffle coats and upturned wellington boots, some with twisty smoking pipes stuck into large jawlines between crooked teeth. Every morning they waited patiently at the door to James Meade's shed, holding warped wheels or rolls of electrical wire or sets of yard lights. Sometimes there were women. One of the school teachers called regularly with her high nelly.

Delia pours dough into a long cake tin at the round table in the front kitchen. Through the tall window, she can see the school teacher standing close to James Meade as he fiddles with her bicycle chain at the shed door. But James Meade seemed to hardly notice her, so absorbed was he in the job at hand. He was doing terrific business. He was a great bicycle mechanic and electrician. But he worked a lot slower now.

James Meade told Delia that he sat on the earth beside the grave where Anthony was buried and cried. He cursed himself he said, for not closing the door properly the night before Anthony went out. He could not sleep. He got up and smoked cigarettes, looking at the street lights in the Bog Road. He was tired in the mornings but he went to eight o'clock Mass and then the graveyard.

Most people who came to James Meade's garage paid by credit. They never paid when he fixed something: they paid on the 'never-never', a month later or two months later. Sometimes they never paid. Sometimes they never paid and kept coming to him to get their bicycles fixed.

Delia told James Meade he was a very good mechanic but he was not a good businessman. Mr Taunton was not a mechanic but he was an able manager. He had opened a shop on Main Street selling discount goods and was said to be making a fortune. If James Meade wanted to be his own boss, let him at it, Mr Taunton was said to have muttered in one of the pubs down the town.

Delia said that maybe James Meade should ask Mr Taunton would he run the bicycle shop again with him as the mechanic. James Meade said he would think about that. But he kept going to Anthony's grave every morning. He began to leave the shed closed until lunch time. He walked out to the lake in the mid-morning. He stood at the edge staring into the deep water.

One day James Meade walked around the front kitchen, clutching a bundle of invoices, a bicycle tyre tube and a spanner. Two customers were waiting for him in the shed. He ran up the stairs looking for his rubber invoice stamp. He found it on the small table in the front bedroom. Beside the green alarm clock, there were a pile of unopened envelopes. He picked them up and opened one as he walked out into the landing. Joseph was playing cowboys on the landing. James Meade stepped to avoid Joseph's sudden leap and tripped on a toy train that Sam had left there. James Meade fell down the stairs, unable to catch the banister, holding onto the spanner and the invoices in one hand, the rubber stamp and the envelopes in the other. As he careered against the front doorjamb, a loose brake wire stabbed James Meade in the right eye.

They gave him a delph eye. The garage closed for good. Every day, James Meade sat at the round table in the front kitchen, smoking cigarettes and reading the newspaper with his left eye. He was afraid, he said, to miss a nut with his sight and his headaches and his mind full of invoices and then somebody's bicycle wheel to fall off or the brakes to fail and them to land in the lake or some other disaster.

Philly and Jack come more often now. Philly's Jack is red-faced when they arrive at eleven o'clock. 'The car was scraped in Galway. Some young bastard hit the mirror. That's the youth of today. The whole thing could cost me two hundred pound.'

'How are you, Mammy?' Philly says.

'Good.' Delia puts the brown kettle on the front left-hand hob. They sit, Delia in her armchair at the red tiled mantelpiece, Philly in the armchair where Mrs Freeley usually sits and Philly's Jack in the two-seater.

'Mammy? You never lit the gas?' Philly gets up and walks over to the cooker. 'Where do you keep the matches?'

'Are you farming away, Jack?' Delia says, after a while.

'Tis hard to make a pound down there,' Philly's Jack says, pulling his collar up around his woollen jumper. His hair is wavy. Philly has cut her hair short now, it is the new style she says.

Delia looks out the tall window. There are no sheets on the washing line today. Philly's Jack drinks his tea and smokes a John Player Blue cigarette which leaves a grey cloud floating near the ceiling in the front kitchen. 'I don't know in the hell. We were going to build on a shed for another couple of cows you know, but tis hard to get the grant nowadays. Such a collection of forms, you know. And interest rates have gone up again.' Philly's Jack says.

'Have they?' Philly says.

'Yes.' Philly's Jack says. 'Everything is going up except beef prices. I'm renting one hundred acres off a neighbour, and the price

of it. Jaysus. He's a robbin' bastard, a robbin' bastard.' Philly's Jack
is drinking more tea. 'We were thinking of planting some of this ele-
phant grass, you know, Delia. Grows to six or eight foot, boy. Great
stuff altogether. But feck it, there is a big outlay so we don't know.'

Rochelle runs into the front kitchen. 'Mammy, there is nothing to
do here.'

'Can't you play with one of the toys in the box room?'

'But I don't like them, mammy…why are we here all day, mammy, can't we just go home?' Rochelle twirls the straps attached to her
summer dress around and around.

'The bastard has hardly any stakes at all around his field, any
stakes at all,' Philly's Jack says.

'Shush, child!' Philly says. 'Go on, we are talking. Go on, I said!'

Rochelle runs out of the front kitchen. Delia makes tea in the
white delph teapot and ham sandwiches at three o'clock. 'No brown
sauce for me,' Philly's Jack says.

Delia's eyes are closing. It is half past eight. Philly's Jack drinks
from another cup of tea. Philly snorts at the round table. Rochelle
sleeps on the two-seater, clutching a doll. She is nine years old now.
'I should have got into pigs by rights. That would have been the right
thing to do. Fecking cows and beef cattle. No money out of it. No
money at all. We'll be out on the street the way things are going.'

'We better be getting home,' Philly says.

'Ha? Hum? I suppose. Where is Rochelle? Hie! Hie! Wake up!'
Philly's Jack shakes Rochelle on the two-seater. Delia looks around
at them gathering their things up. They have two large bags of shopping which they had with them when they came. Philly and Philly's
Jack wave as they drive off down the Bog Road. Delia looks around
the quiet street and closes the door.

7.

The next day Delia waddles around the house on the Bog Road. She walks through the front hall and looks into the front room. She goes upstairs and stands on the landing, looking into the box room. She looks into the back room and the front bedroom. She goes back downstairs and looks into the back kitchen and turns her head to the front kitchen. She walks to the bathroom and looks in through the doorway. She turns and walks to the sideboard under the drinks cabinet beside the round table. She opens the middle drawer and takes out a white cardboard box with the word 'Belvedere' written across it in an elegant style. Within is a pad of heavy cream sheets, several white envelopes, a blue lined sheet, two black ball-point pens and two pencils, a pencil sharpener and an eraser.

Delia sits at the round table and slides the blue lined sheet under the first white sheet.

'Dear Megan,' she writes. She tears this sheet away and crumbles it into a ball. She writes on the next sheet:

> The round table - The front kitchen.
> The glory hole - Under the stairs.
> The coat stand - The front hall.
> The piano - The front room.
> The box room - single bed.
> The back room - double bed.

Delia sits on the bed in the back room. The springs creak underneath. James Meade had gotten a deal on three mattresses once. At the top, under the pillows, is a sewn-on label with the legend: 'Sleep right, wake up bright.' Here all of the children slept, apart from some of the boys who used the box room and Barbara who was always in the front bedroom until she grew up. The tall shiny teak wardrobe stands in the corner. Delia looks around, lost, trying to find the door, peering forward. She looks at the cracks in the ceiling above and the dull daylight which lies across it in a soft beam.

On the locker, by the bed, there is a small statue of Our Lady, with her hands outstretched, both palms open, her eyes a light blue. The face smiles. Our Lady grows to the size of a normal person. Our Lady speaks to Delia but Delia cannot understand what it is Our Lady is saying to her. The language sounds to Delia very elegant and very beautiful.

Delia falls asleep on the bed in the back room in the house in the Bog Road. There are wild horses galloping along a sandy beach, waves on the ocean froth and the three Jacks stand in a little boat, laughing, and all of Delia's many children tug at her skirt on a small bare island and James Meade sits on a wicker chair asking, 'Where is the bleddy paper?' and Delia walks along the shore, her toes sinking in through the grains and the sand is warm as the sun shines on her forehead and she wakes up and it is morning again.

Sometimes other visitors come into the front bedroom as Delia sleeps. Pope John Paul II, St Luke, St Anthony. Jesus Christ comes another night. He is Jesus Christ, Delia is sure, even though he looks nothing like his Sacred Heart portrait. She cannot understand a word these figures say, they speak in a different language. There is a certain gentleness in the way they speak, as though they are friendly to her, it doesn't seem to matter that she cannot understand them, it doesn't seem too important. The fact that they are there and they are there in a way she can recognise makes her feel relaxed and helps her to sleep. For the worst fear is that she wouldn't wake up at all and that she was going to be asleep forever. That is the biggest fear she had.

One night, one of the figures asks to marry Delia. 'To marry me?' Delia says. 'But to who?'

'To me, of course, Delia,' Jesus Christ says, hopping around the room in his dark suit and his grey hair. He grabs Delia by the waist. She tries to shout some words, but she cannot form them, only a gurgling sound comes. Jesus Christ ran out the door.

Every morning at seven, Delia turns on the immersion, pushing up a red switch within the yellow patterned tiles near the cooker in the back kitchen. She takes her pink tablet at this time now also. She chews her cornflakes and drinks from a cup at the round table in the front room. The tea is cold.

Delia takes sheets from the odd shaped linen press above the stairs soffit. She takes the old sheets off the beds and puts the fresh ones on. She covers them with the other clean sheets. She smoothes each blanket back onto each bed. She tucks in the corners under the mattress. She takes the other sheets off the ground and brings them downstairs and puts them on the floor beside the bath. She takes out a

63

box of washing powder from under the sink in the back kitchen. She sprinkles the flakes from the box over each sheet as she holds it across the water in the bath. One by one she washes each sheet, scrubbing it with a hard brush. She rinses it in another basin of water which she has filled beside the bath. Then wringing it, she brings that sheet out to the washing line. She repeats this with the other five sheets.

Six sheets, three beds, every day Delia washes six, she has twelve sheets in all. Delia sits on her armchair beside the red tiled mantelpiece and looks out through the tall window in the front kitchen at the sheets billowing on the washing line and in between Our Lady stands on the table. Delia opens her mouth a little and stops breathing for a second. She gets up off the armchair, goes out through the back kitchen, through the bathroom, out the back door and takes down all of the sheets off the line. She brings them back into the bathroom. She fills the bath and begins to wash the sheets again, one by one. As she washes, she puts them in a pile on the toilet seat.

St Francis of Assisi stands behind Delia and puts his arm on her shoulder and she looks around and St Francis has a band of hair around his crown and wears a brown wool habit. Delia understands nothing St Francis says, but he says everything is going to be alright.

Delia goes into the back kitchen and puts the brown kettle on the front right-hand hob. She turns on the gas at the collar of the cylinder beside the humming fridge. She sits on the armchair at the red tiled mantelpiece. The sheets drip onto the floor of the bathroom. There is a strong smell. Delia feels warm. She falls asleep. Delia is walking along the side of the road, the straps of her sandals are cutting into her ankle. Maisie, laughing, turns to Delia, her eyes are a light blue, teeth straight, long brown hair lifting in the light breeze.

'We better get back, Ma will be waiting,' Delia is saying.

'Ah, Dee, go on…' Maisie says.

The green stems of the flowers shudder. The bees buzz nearby, sucking nectar. Delia sees one on a daisy. Delia and Maisie watch the bee. It flies into the air. Delia jumps back a step.

'Watch out, Dee,' Maisie says, laughing. Delia laughs too. A thumping sound breaks the quiet of the day. Wheels grind on the dusty road. There is a beeping noise. The banker's son drives, the vehicle swerves, the boy's mouth hangs open, his eyes are red in the wind.

'Get ourra the way, brakes!' the boy says, standing up, still gripping the steering wheel. The motor car jolts, turned wheels skid along the ground. Maisie tries to jump in but hits Delia and falls back into the path of the motor-car. The front left-hand wheel knocks Maisie to the ground. Her head hits the hard clay with a smack. The motor car runs into a stone wall a few yards down the road. A hissing noise comes from beneath the steaming bonnet. The banker's son is gasping. Maisie lies still on the road. Delia looks at the growing pool of blood around her head. If Delia wasn't standing in Maisie's way, Maisie wouldn't have been hit. The noise repeats now in Delia's head: smack-smack, smack-smack-smack, smack-smack, smack-smack-smack. The smack becomes a dull thud. Thud-thud, thud-thud-thud, thud-thud, thud-thud-thud. There is a knock at the door. Now Mrs Freeley is at the cooker turning off the gas.

'Hello, Delia, how are you today?' Dr Wilson says.
    'Not too bad, Doctor.'
    'And how are all your family?'
    'Very good.'
    'That's great. So what can I do?'
    'Well, I'm still having a bit of trouble.'
    'What kind of trouble, Delia?
    'I'm still getting…a bit forgetful.' Delia says.
    'Hmm. How are you sleeping?'
    'I can't sleep much. I left the gas on the last evening. Agnes next door says I'll have to get an electric cooker.'
    'I see. Are you happy to stay living alone, Delia? You have a daughter nearby, do you?'
    'I do, but she has a young family. I wouldn't like to be in the way.'
    'Okay. I'm going to put you on Chlordiazepoxide. It's another sedative. It should calm you a bit at night.'
    'Will I keep taking the other ones?'
    'Yes. We'll try that for two weeks and see how you go.'
    'Thank you, Doctor.'
    At ten o'clock Delia takes one of the red tablets and tries to sleep. She twists and turns for three hours. In the middle of the night there is a noise in the front bedroom. Delia opens her eyes and looks at the base of the bed. A silver winged creature stands there, with arms

folded. It begins to laugh, laugh loudly. Delia looks straight at it until it disappears. Delia lies down and closes her eyes.

Delia stops taking both pink and red tablets the next day. The visions fade. Delia sleeps. It is daytime. She is going to bed at eleven in the morning. The clock with the Roman numerals in the front kitchen is wrong. Delia takes out the battery, looks at it. She puts it back in again.

Delia is dreaming. It is a restless dream, one that follows her sleep pattern around like a hungry dog. She is standing in a bright hall, with rows of young men along the sides, dressed in dark wool robes. They stare ahead, their faces neither happy nor sad, friendly nor aloof. Their mouths are closed, their eyes are unblinking. Their jaws are cleanshaven.

Above Delia is a glass roof where the sun or some light shines through. At one end of the hall a figure dressed in an intricately patterned dark shawl sits on a gold throne.

Delia wears a white dress, her hair tied back with a white ribbon, her face wrinkle-free, her lips pursed together. She feels young and happy. It seems to be a time of some other century, of some other place. That she is not a part of, yet she feels a part of. Her glass shoes connect crisply with the marble floor. She is walking, yet she is not moving. Nothing moves in this place, everything is still.

Delia continues to walk, still she does not move. There is something familiar about the place, even though she recognises nothing. Everything is white, everything is black. She is alone, she is in company. She seems to feel that James Meade is near, or at least something like James Meade. Perhaps the real James Meade, the James she never knew, the James she loved, the James she knew.

Delia's thoughts are uncontrollable now, they run away, tearing from the maypole in her mind and scampering out into the abyss and doing whatever it is they please. This makes Delia uncomfortable, vulnerable. She is exposed when her thoughts are no longer her own. They leap out through her ear. They materialise into little winged creatures, with mischievous eyes and triangular faces. They cackle, but the sound they make is silent within the hall. They dance in the mid-air, waltzing with each other and laughing at Delia's efforts to gather them up and put them back into her head.

The lines of young men ignore this behaviour and the figure in the throne nods. Delia feels flustered now as she tries to catch these creatures. She picks up a few of them and returns them to inside her head, but the others evade her and she runs around the hall trying to grab them, trying, and reaching and then the dream washes itself into the blackness of awareness, the world destabilised, the hall evaporates into a waxy paint which her subconscious had sprayed onto the canvas of her mind and Delia falls as though from a cliff, she is dropping with increasing speed, her body a thing of the past, there is only her now, there is only her being, herself, her mind, she knows not what vehicle she lives in but its seems to be the best, the most beautiful she ever was, on her wedding day, with clear blue eyes, her sandy hair tied back, a flower on her breast, a white dress and a glittering happiness somewhere in her heart.

Delia drops in this way, seeing her mother and father waving from a cave on the way down, with her sisters, Maisie and Kathleen and James Meade is there too, waving from a lower cave, waving. They all seem so happy and even she is not worried about falling, she thought falling off a cliff would be terrifying, yet it is not, it is somehow liberating, she enjoys the feeling, but now she sees the ground, the hard immovable surface coming closer and there is no one now in the caves on the cliff face waving at her, she is alone, she must meet the ground alone, the birds above her sing, she wishes she could fly now, that she could glide away from the ground which seems to be her destiny, there does not look to be any way out and she drops faster and faster and the ground is almost upon her.

It is morning. The sky is cloudy. In the back kitchen, Delia fills the white plastic kettle that someone gave her and plugs it into the socket amongst the yellow patterned tiles on the wall. A red light comes on below the handle. Delia does not know if this means it is on or if the kettle is overheating. She unplugs the white plastic kettle.

Delia takes the brown kettle from the first press under the counter beside the cooker and fills it with water. She takes out the box of matches from beside the plates in the first press above the counter and strikes a match, but the front right-hand hob will not light. She checks the dial. The gas is on. She looks to the other side of the humming fridge beside the cooker and sees the gas collar hanging down against the yellow patterned tiles. The orange gas cylinder is not there anymore. Kevin's lad removed the cylinder, carrying it out the back door and wheeling it away in a rusting trolley. Delia plugs the white plastic kettle in.

The doorbell rings. Thomas stands on the path with a cigarette smouldering between his teeth. His lips are creased into a smile. His blue battered suitcase stands on the path. He holds a bunch of petunias in his right hand. 'For you, ma, it's Mother's Day, so I hears. I got the early train,' Thomas says. 'I was gathering up the money for the ticket and I said I'll bring you down something for Mother's Day because I saw an advert for it in the paper.'

He walks in, kissing Delia on the cheek as he passes her. His lips are dry, his breath of whiskey and gravy.

'Arrah, bleddy commercialism that's what it is, still, I said I would, so there they are,' Thomas says, as he takes off his long grey overcoat and hangs it on the coat stand. He goes upstairs carrying his suitcase, whistling.

'Still no word of Barry?' Delia says, loud enough for her voice to travel up the stairs.

'That bleddy woman,' Thomas mutters in the back room.

Delia smells the petunias and smiles. She turns and walks down the front hall to the front kitchen. She leaves the petunias on their side in their clear plastic packet of water on the round table and goes over to the sink in the back kitchen. Underneath, she takes out a tall glass vase and half-fills it with water. She goes out to the front room. She looks around the front room for some time.

Thomas stands at the counter in the back kitchen. 'Who got you the breakfast cooker?'

On the counter is a small portable cooker with two panels on top and a grilling area beneath. It is plugged into the socket within the yellow patterned tiles beside the plug for the white plastic kettle. Delia does not know who brought the breakfast cooker.

'We'll cook the dinner on it, I suppose, ma, hah? Safer than the gas anyways.' Thomas walks into the front kitchen. 'Jays ma, you have the placed soaked! Why did you lave the flowers flat on the table!'

At one o'clock, Delia and Thomas sit at the round table eating bacon, cabbage and new potatoes. 'I won't be here long.' Thomas says, between mouthfuls. He drinks from the glass of milk. 'I bought a donkey above and Jimmy Patch is bringing her down for me today. I'm mating the fella is buying it in Packie's after a while. Have you any YR?'

Thomas shakes the brown bottle of sauce. 'She's a great little donkey,' he says. 'Just two years old. Bought her for fifteen on the never-never in Dublin and Johnny McDonagh will pay twenty-five down here. I gave Patch two quid to bring her down tomorrow. He has an empty trailer coming every second day. Brings pullets up to the farmers in North Dublin, y'see.'

He clears the plate, smacks his lips, finishes the milk and sits back, looking out the tall window at the sheets lifting in the breeze.

Delia takes their plates and washes them in the sink in the back kitchen. She hears Thomas crack a match and cigarette smoke lifts around the front kitchen. 'Are you sure he'll buy it off you?' Delia says.

'Of course he will,' Thomas says. 'It's still a fairly good deal. I'll be sitting pretty this evening, ma!'

At five o'clock Delia sets the table. The breakfast cooker is slower than the gas. Thomas had said he would be back with his winnings in plenty of time. But his egg goes cold in the egg cup and the toast goes hard.

Delia wakens when Thomas comes home, pounding the stairs. James Meade is not there beside her anymore.

'Bastard!' Thomas says. 'Fucking bastard.' He leaves early the next morning. There are drops of dried blood on the stairs.

8.

'Philly come in out of the sun, you will get burnt,' Delia says to Michelle, who is standing on the threshold of the back door. Delia can see her blonde hair through the tall window.

'Are you okay, mammy?' Margaret says.

Margaret drinks a cup of tea at the round table and she looks at Delia and she looks at Jack. Jack sits on the two-seater with his legs spread apart and his belly flopping down over his groin. He picks his nose and rubs his stockinged feet together. His shoes are beside his feet and a smell from them floats around the front kitchen.

Delia is looking around for Philly who was playing in the front kitchen a few moments earlier. She sees Margaret staring at Jack. Delia looks out the window. 'Jack?'

'Yes, love?'

'Are you?'

'Huh?'

'Are you?' Margaret nods at Jack. Delia watches the washing line, a thin stripe dancing up and down across the glass. There are no sheets there today.

'Oh,' Jack says. 'Well…Delia…Ehheemm. You know at work, in the department, we are coming across a lot of civil cases to do with …well, with wills not being sorted out right, and well I was, we were worried, if you…'

'What's that, Jack?'

'If you had…you and Jim…'

'Oh, for God's sake, did you and daddy make a will, mammy?' Margaret says. Delia looks around the front kitchen at the people sitting there.

'Daddy made one,' Delia says. There are people there, there are no people there. A folder is opened in an office, thick cream sheets of paper, signed with a ballpoint pen, there are laughs and smiles and handshakes. There is a dark-haired man wearing a pinstripe suit, there is a walnut desk with green leather panels. On top, a golden lamp with a solid green shade.

'Oh? And what did he do?'

'What did you say, Philly?'

'It's Margaret, mammy, Jesus!'

'Don't take the Lord's name in vain, good girl!'

Delia is at the carnival clutching a big red balloon outside the coastal town. Her mother brings her and Maisie there after Sunday mass. A young man and a young woman walk past. The woman lightly elbows the man. They both giggle. Delia tightens her grip of her mother's hand. 'I want to get married when I grow up, mammy,' Delia says.

'We may as well go. We'll see you next week, mammy. Michelle!'

'Next week?' Jack says.

'Yeah, sure, Jesus. We'll have to get something organised.'

'Like what?'

They continue their conversation in the front hall and then the front door closes and Delia is alone.

Mary's Jack is in the shed at the bottom of the garden. Delia can see him from her armchair beside the red tiled mantelpiece. She did not hang any sheets out today. She took the sheets off the beds and left them on the bath. They are still there. Mary kneels at the press doors under the counter beside the cooker in the back kitchen. She wipes with a J-cloth. 'You'd want to change these units, ma. Jack might be able to pick you up something somewhere,' she says.

'What is he doing in the shed?' Delia asks.

'God knows. Jack!' Mary shouts from the back door.

'What is it?'

'What are you doing there?'

'I was looking for a spanner,' Mary's Jack says, walking down the path, carrying a paint can.

'That doesn't look like a spanner,' Mary says, as Jack walks past her into the back kitchen.

'Well, fair play to you woman!' Mary's Jack says. 'I have a bitteen of a job and I need a drop of gloss, Delia. I might take this can, is that aright?'

'Well, Thomas that bought that. I'd say he is finished with it.'

'What is that for?' Mary says.

'Arrah, that Munnelly woman's skirting, you know. I ran out and I'm not buying another fucking can. Hard to get a bitch like that to pay the first price, never mind add-ons.'

'Shush!' Delia says.

In the evening they sit at the round table. In the centre, there is a large dish with a roast chicken. Jack carves the bird up, placing portions on each plate. 'This was a big chicken, you got Mary. Was it in Kevin's you bought it?' Delia says.

'No, down the town. I wanted one to feed five. Two portions for himself.'

'You're funny, woman,' Jack says. 'Very tasty, though.' He tears meat from a leg with his protruding teeth.

'Better than the dinners at work,' Mary says.

'Are you busy there, now Mary?'

'Oh busy enough. But I don't mind the work. The worst is when you get to know them and then they…'

'Depressing place, it is,' Mary's Jack says. He pours Coca-Cola down his throat and makes a loud gulp. 'Hmm. Don't know how you work in it. Smell a' piss and everything.'

'Shush,' Delia says.

'What do you mean, it's not clean?'

'I didn't say that love, you know.'

'There is no smell of urine in there. That is the chlorine you smell!'

'The what?

'The chlorine.'

'The stuff in swimming pools? I know the difference–'

'It's clean, and don't be making remarks like that.'

'What? I just said–'. On the Grunow radio, there is an important announcement.

'Shush…listen,' Delia says.

'German forces have invaded Poland and its planes have bombed Polish cities, including the capital, Warsaw. The attack comes without any warning or declaration of war. Britain and France have mobilised their forces and are preparing to wage war on Germany for the second time this century. The Taoiseach has made no comment yet on the matter.'

'That's it now, ration books again,' James Meade says, crossing his legs. He takes a final pull on his cigarette and stubs it in the ashtray on the round table. He finishes his cup of tea and leans back on the chair.

'It mightn't come to that.' Delia ties a fresh cloth nappy around Philly's waist. 'Now pettin',' she whispers. 'Will they come here?'

'Who?'

'The Germans?'

'Not at all, woman. What would they want with this bleddy place? Sure every man is leaving.'

'There you go, lovin',' Delia says, tightening the soft blue blanket around Philly in the pram in the front kitchen.

'I've a splitting headache, I'm going up,' James Meade says.

'She looks lively yet, I'll wait a while.'

'Alright.' James Meade gets up. 'It's his anniversary tomorrow,' he says, at the door into the front hall. He looks out the tall window. 'Eight years gone. Imagine.'

'You don't want a Mass, Jim?'

'God, no. Do you?'

'No.'

'Let's say no more about it, then.'

James Meade walks out through the front hall and up the stairs. There is a clink as he takes out his false eye, drops it into the silver bowl beside the green alarm clock on the small table and climbs into bed.

They are all going to the seaside. Barbara is packing Delia's blue canvas bag with a grey flask of tea and a Clingfilm wrapped bundle of ham sandwiches. Delia walks around in a circle in the front kitchen. Children make loud thudding noises upstairs in the box room. Aidan scratches his chin through his goatee as he reads the Sunday newspaper. 'Just a couple of hours, Mammy. Over to Old Head,' Barbara says.

They get into Aidan's blue Renault 12. Delia sits in the front passenger seat. She watches the Bog Road zip past as the car speeds to the junction. Aidan turns right, drives past the school for children with special needs, out the Coast Road. The countryside flows along Delia's eye line in a blur of colour. As a child she walked miles everywhere. Her and Maisie. Three miles into town to get Pear's soap. 'Come on, Dee!' Maisie says. 'It'll be closed by the time we get there!' They hold hands as they skip along the boreen.

The beach is crowded. Families argue about the best place to lay out their towels and blankets and where to position their deckchairs. Barbara and Aidan do not argue. They both agree to set up near the road. 'Keep away from the water!' Barbara says to the children who run around on the sand.

'We really should bring them to swimming lessons,' Aidan says, as he spreads out a blanket on the sand.

'I don't know! The water is dangerous. I never liked it. Anyone can be drowned in an instant!'

The boy sits on the sand, reading a book. The girl kneels beside him, digging with her fingers. Delia walks around in a circle.

'We should have brought some kind of chair for Mammy,' Barbara says.

The baby cries. Barbara kneels at the carrycot. She peels back the blankets. Aidan sits on the sand and opens the newspaper.

'He's done a nappy and I never brought anything with me!' Barbara says. 'We'll have to go home again. I can't leave him like this.'

Aidan pushes his lips together. He folds the newspaper. 'Right,' he says, a wisp of his comb-over has slid across his face.

The boy walks around the house in the Bog Road, peers into each room from the doorway, goes up and down the stairs. In the front kitchen, Barbara sits sketching at the round table. Aidan slouches on the two-seater, reading the newspaper. The baby sleeps in his carrycot in the middle of the room. In the yard, the girl runs around with the black cat. When a dog barks from the back road, the girl runs inside. 'Terrified of dogs,' Barbara says.

The boy comes into the front kitchen with a large book. He sits at the round table across from Barbara, slowly turning the pages. There are drawings of animals dressed as humans, on trains, buses, working at road works and in houses, cooking and watching television.

Aidan turns a page of the newspaper. Delia sits on her armchair beside the red tiled mantelpiece. She looks out the tall window at the sun's rays breaking through the clouds. She has not put out any sheets today.

'Have you a room for me out there?' Delia says.

'What's that Mammy?' Barbara looks up from her drawing. She has Aidan's profile in place; the eyes, the lips and the nose. She is just shading in the crown of his head.

'In the Country, ye would have a room for me?'

'Yes, Mammy, do you want to come out for a night?'

There is now a lot of activity in the house on the Bog Road. At about half nine in the morning, on more than one occasion, Delia is disturbed from washing the sheets in the bathroom or sweeping the yard to be led by the arm out of the house in the Bog Road and into a motor car. The people in the motor car talk to each other. There are no children present. Delia watches the streets move by quickly. They arrive at different offices in different parts of town. Different men, with different suits and different smiles. They all shake Delia's hand. The others explain what is going on. Delia does not know what is going on. Light white sheets of typed paper are produced. Delia is told to sign her name on the papers with a ballpoint pen. The men smile, the others smile. 'Sound mind,' Delia hears.

'Thank you.'

'Thank you, Mr Stephens.'

Delia wants an ice cream. She looks around for Maisie but cannot find her at the carnival. The office is cold. The hotel is ready for James Meade and her.

The Meades walk along the soft carpet, golden framed paintings of landscapes hang on the beige walls. They sit at a table with a sherry and a Jameson. They hold hands on a salty promenade. There is a four-poster bed. Delia looks out the window of a bedroom with a view of the sea.

James Meade stands at a hotel reception with a fistful of dollars. 'You'll take these?'

'No problem, Mr Meade,' the manager says. 'It was a wonderful wedding present, Megan,' Delia writes on her Belvedere writing paper at the square table in the front kitchen of the house on Ryan's Road.

'Had you a good time?' the manager says.

'Wonderful time,' James Meade says.

The man leads Delia through a hallway to a room with a strong smell of wood. The man stretches his arm out around the room. The brass handles reflect Delia's image. The inside is lined with light blue material. It feels soft. But underneath is hard.

'Figures or plain,' the man is saying. It is difficult to see, it is difficult to hear, it is difficult to remember, it is difficult to forget.
Mr Stephens is shaking his head. Somebody is getting agitated, Delia can hear a quiver in their voice. 'She said it to us the last day, didn't you, mammy?'

'What was that, Delia?' Mr Stephens is saying.

Delia lies on the white sheet in the front bedroom in the house in Ryan's Road.

'The first one is the worst, you'll see, ma'am. After that they'll just fly out! Almost as aisy as they went in!' The green-eyed woman with curly black hair winks and laughs, squeezing a towel in her hand. Agony surges through Delia's body, as though a beam of white heat ran through her, she could not think, or speak.

At the front door, Mr Stephens holds a grey folder in his left hand. 'Who?' Delia is saying.

'Liam Stephens, Delia. How are you?'

Delia plugs in the white plastic kettle. She takes out the white delph teapot from the middle press under the counter in the back kitchen. Mr Stephens sits in Delia's armchair at the red tiled mantelpiece. Delia brings the white delph teapot over to the round table in the front kitchen. The silver sugar bowl is already in the centre. She pours two cups. 'Milk, Mr Stephens?'

'Just a small drop please, and one sugar, Delia,' Mr Stephens says, staring into the empty fireplace. Delia hands Mr Stephens the cup and a small plate of arrowroot biscuits. 'Thank you.'

Delia sits where Mrs Freeley usually sits. The front room does not look familiar from this angle. Delia gazes behind Mr Stephens, at the wall where the clock with Roman numerals hangs beside the golden framed photograph of Delia, James Meade and Barbara Meade. The two-seater is vacant. 'It's not often I have a law man here,' Delia says.

'How are you getting on, Delia?'

'Good, Mr Stephens.'

'Please, Liam is fine. Ah yes, things are gone to hell in this country, Delia. Sure there is no work for anyone.'

'Well, I suppose a lawyer will always be busy.'

Mr Stephens sips his tea. 'You'd be surprised, very surprised.'

'It's hard for everyone in tough times, Jimmy used to say,' Delia says. Her tea is cold.

'Ah yes.' Mr Stephens puts his cup beside the plate of arrowroot biscuits on the black hearth. 'Jim was a great character. In hard luck, that was all. It seems like only yesterday he passed on.'

Mr Stephens is gone. Delia sits alone in the front kitchen in the house in the Bog Road.

Delia – carted up the road – down the road – into Mr Stephens' – out of Mr Stephens' – down the road – back to the house in the Bog Road. Stacks of paper, handwritten, typed, shiny black hardback covers. Different offices. Different men. Carpet smell. A group around a table. Pen on the desk. Expensive fountain. Delia looks around for the round table. The Challen Evans miniature piano is at the back of Mr Stephens' office. 'Are you okay, Delia?' someone says.

A light through the window, early in the morning. Late now. Mass time. Saturday night. A group around a table. Not the round table. A square table. A rectangular table. A leather backed seat. A man in a pinstripe suit, Mr Stephens. Strange foreign grey words.

Foreign cold distant words beside homely warm names. James Meade, of sound mind and body. Latin words on framed scrolls, at school, a teacher, a priest speaking Latin, in the cold marble of Sunday morning, shouting, roaring, louder and louder.

109, Bog Road. A town. A country. A world. A place to be called home. Scrambled egg with sugar, something wrong, something wrong. Delia turns and twists in the chair as though tied down at the arm rests. Arms tied, legs tied, rocking in an armchair. What they have, what we have, what they have. Who has what? Delia is confused. Good. All good.

Making a jigsaw, putting the wooden pieces in, a click when each segment drops into place and soon the picture is complete.

Inside, outside. Inside, outside. Warm and cold. In and out. Clear water on a summer's day. Water stained with a tea bag and swirling to the top like brown and milk expanding, like smoke clouds from a silent explosion, through the water and pog, from the insertion of bread, thickening the liquid to custard and then semolina and then glue and then concrete, thickening and setting.

Soon there will be a glittering mosaic and it will all become clear and sharp and everything will be wonderful. Nobody speaks to Delia in the room with Mr Stephens.

The day continues – the day ends – there is more – there is no more – there are crowds of people – there are people coming in and talking and going out.

Delia is at the red tiled mantelpiece, sitting in the armchair, looking out the tall window over the yard. There are no sheets hanging on the washing line. Delia is being led through a doorway. She does not need help, she needs help. There are suitcases on the brown patterned carpet. Someone is going on holidays, there are people, there are many people, there are no people. Delia is lost, Delia is found, somebody leads Delia, nobody leads Delia.

'Are you alright, Delia?' Aidan says, stroking his chin through his goatee. Delia does not know where Aidan is. She does not know where she is. Now she is at Mr Stephens' office, staring at the 'V' between his eyebrows. That was how Mr Taunton looked, James

Meade used to say, a very obvious 'V' between the eyebrows. Mr Taunton dead for years now. Everyone dead for years now. 'Are you alright, mammy?'

Someone comes, someone goes. Mrs Freeley is holding a bag, shaking Delia's hand. Delia does not know why. Delia cannot find her shoe, she is looking for her shoe, people are in the way, she puts out her hand to get to the top of the water, she cannot breathe, cannot reach the surface, cannot reach the floor underneath, here in a queer middle place, struggling, neither roof above nor floor below, water going down her throat, into her lungs. Delia scrapes someone, there is blood, there are voices, it is lost, there is light, there is dark, the door of 109 closes.

There is a bright light hovering at the end of the Bog Road as Aidan's Renault 12 accelerates down the street. At the junction, Delia looks right, from the back seat, through the glass at the school for children with special needs. Beyond is the Coast Road which leads to the seaside where she once lived in a stone cottage and slept every night with Maisie in an attic under the thatch where they could hear the waves. They turn left, driving out the country road and the light goes out.

9.

Delia sits in the room in the Country. She can hear voices from beyond the door, a man and woman speaking, Barbara and Aidan. The voices are muffled but Delia can hear some words. 'Wet…yes…yes…number…forms.'

Children play nearby, in another room. Delia's rosary beads, false teeth in a cloudy glass and statue of Our Lady are on a half-moon table near the window. A vase of plastic anemones is in the middle of the table, near the window board. The curtains are not quite together. One of them is draped awkwardly around the vase. Delia is worried it will knock it over.

A cane walking stick rests against the side of the bed. Delia's fingers are intertwined on her lap. A bullock tears grass in the field outside and stares in through the curtains.

One wall is papered with cartoon characters, Mickey Mouse, Donald Duck and Goofy, they stand around something, Delia cannot quite make it out. The characters are not smiling. There is a problem in the scene. It is replicated throughout the wallpaper. There is a large poster on the ceiling, directly over Delia's bed. It is of a kitten, covered up to its head with a pink blanket, one paw just over the top. The kitten is asleep.

The floor is covered in beige linoleum. The tall shiny teak wardrobe from the back room in the house in the Bog Road is stood in a recessed section. It is tilted forward slightly. The door is open. Within are Delia's clothes: skirts, blouses, underwear on the shelf at the top, her brown shoes and her green faded cardigan at the bottom beside her blue canvas bag. Only her gabardine jacket hangs on the rail.

Delia grips the grey aluminium armrests of the chair. It has a compartment beneath the seat 'for emergencies', Barbara had said. On the back of the chair hangs her green wool coat. There is a plastic potty underneath the bed.

Delia does not know what is beyond the door of the bedroom. She only knows what is within the walls. The room could be on an empty planet. She can see the bullock chewing grass now, but this too could be an illusion. Delia does not trust what she sees. Delia believes what her hands can feel. She grips the armrests tighter.

Delia's black bag is on a white fridge which hums at the end of the bed. She gets up slowly and walks down to it, opening the door. Inside, there are three pizzas, a tub of flora margarine and three two litre cartons of milk. She closes the fridge door and opens her black handbag. Within, there is an address book, some elastic bands, a ball-point pen, a large comb, loose hairgrips. In a pocket on the inside are pieces of paper: butcher counter tickets, receipts, shopping lists. At the bottom of the handbag is her green purse. She opens it. There are a few brown coins inside.

Delia opens the room door, turning the brass doorknob. She wobbles. She waddles to the bed, taking up the cane walking stick, fitting her hands around it, prodding it to the floor. It makes her walk easier.

In a long hall, a boy and a girl are pulling each other in and out of a room. Delia looks to the left to a door with a glass panel above it. She opens the door and it leads into a small odd shaped area with more doors, including an external door. Barbara and Aidan can be heard more clearly now. Delia follows the voices, turning the brass doorknob to the right.

It is a kitchen. Aidan sits on a square table in a chair against a door. Barbara is at a range, holding a poker. 'Mammy, are you alright?' Barbara says.

'Yes,' Delia says. She walks into the kitchen. To the left is another fridge, a washing machine and a narrow compartment under a white counter next to a sink and draining board over a group of pine presses and drawers. Over the sink is a long high window facing onto a network of green fields. The narrow compartment's door is open, within a box of Brillo pads, beyond there is a black void.

'Do you want a cup of tea?'

'Yes.' Delia sits on a chair in between the square table at the pine presses. She pulls out the middle drawer, cutlery rattles.

'What are you looking for, mammy?' Barbara says.

'I can't find me pension book...' Delia says.

Delia stands on the road outside the house in the Country. She wears her green wool coat and in her right hand carries her blue canvas bag. Her black handbag is on her shoulder. A motor car comes along. She puts her hand out, her thumb pointing to the sky. The motor car slows down.

'Hello there,' the driver says.

Barbara comes from the garden. 'Where are you going, mammy? It's alright, Micksie, it's just me mother.'

'Oh, I see, no problem. How is everyone?'

'Fine, and all of your lot?'

'Great, great. See you, Barbara.'

'See you Micksie, thanks.' The motor car drives away.

'I wanted a lift home,' Delia says.

The boy and his sister are in Delia's room playing with a train. Delia lies in the bed. Delia does not know how long she has been in the Country. She was born in a village near the sea. They do not have a farm. Daddy works for another man, saving hay and turf in the summer, feeding stock with the hay and delivering the turf in the winter.

'You should have gone into them, ya bleddy gom!' Delia's mother says, flicking a torn cloth at a fly in their stone cottage. A pot hangs within a blackened stone fireplace. Turf smoulders underneath. 'We wouldn't be answering to that fella now! The days of bleeding landlords are over in this country, except for asses like Tom O'Grady!'

'They wouldn't give me the papers, I tell you, woman!' Delia's father says. Delia and Maisie run outside and play hide-and-seek in the sun. Delia is the first to hide and she skips down the path of flattened dying grass, out the white front gate and down the clay track, running as fast as she can, laughing at the energy of it, over a stile and across the lush green meadow, the scent wafts up her nose, and she lies on the ground amongst the thick green stems, smiling at her concealment.

From the cottage, she can hear voices. 'Better off in America!'

'Shut up woman!'

'Scared of your own shadow!'

'Shut up woman!'

It is three o'clock. Delia stands at the sink in the kitchen in the house in the Country, washing a plate. The water runs slowly from the tap into the half-filled sink. A tea bag and part of a potato are stuck at the plug hole and the water gradually soaks through and down the drain. The water level does not rise. The water level does not drop. Delia rinses the plate and places it on the draining board and takes another plate from the first press over the square table by the door and begins washing it. Outside, clouds are lit by the moon, dawn has not yet arrived.

Delia sits in her room. The door is closed. The doors are different in the house in the Country. They shut with a click and bang unlike the soft thud of the glossed latches in the house in the Bog Road. The doors in the house in the Bog Road were rarely closed, except the door into the glory hole. The doors in the Country are usually closed. The brass knobs have a little button to press for locking but that has been disabled on Delia's door.

The noise of the children often comes from one of the rooms along the long hall. 'Give me it!'

'No!'

'Give me, I said!'

'No! Ow. Ow. Mammy!'

Delia looks at the door.

'Get off me! Mammy!'

'Give it to me!'

Another day.

'You seek and I'll hide.'

'But I seeked the last time!'

'Yeah, but you just hide in silly places!'

They use a different tone when they visit Delia in her room. 'Hello granny.'

'Here is your tea, granny.'

There is some hesitance in their voices, some slow tone, as though they are talking to someone simple-minded or to a baby. Fragments of sound come through the door to Delia's room at night as she lies in the bed. Adult conversations in the kitchen.   'Money...there is...looking at that...'

'Yeah...mmm...mmm...okay...mmm.'

'Course...'

'Mmm.'

'Over and then...and ...if we could...'

'Yeah...maybe.'

'Others...Philomena.'

Delia lies in the bed. Maisie lies dead, laid out, mother crying, father looking left, then right, people rushing, sitting, over, over, dead, final, final, end, the end, the end. Candles, incense, church, readings, doll, white coffin, clay, ground, the ground. Dark pub, stout, sweat, cigarette smoke, heat, cold. Over, over.

Delia can hear the water flowing along the pipes and into the radiator underneath the window. She hears it dripping in and slowly filling to a certain level. After a length of time, it empties, then it re-fills and then re-empties and then re-fills and then re-empties and then re-fills. Heat radiates. Beyond the ceiling, there is a scuffle, something moves in the void above.

The floors are concrete in the house in the Country. They do not shake like the timber floors in the house in the Bog Road. They do not give to footfall. They feel different to walk on, as Delia mooches around the house alone during the morning when everyone is gone, children gone to school, baby at a nursery, Aidan out farming, Barbara at college, studying for something. It is quiet at night. Cars rarely pass. The silence is long. Some nights Delia cannot sleep, seeking the comforting drone of traffic in the Bog Road. The early morning deliveries to Kevin's. The voice of the bread man. 'How are ye, Kevin! Fifty white, twenty brown, yeah? Sixteen cakes, uh?'

Delia had always wanted a big garden and there is ample room around the house in the Country. She steps outside this morning, the air cold into her lungs. Aidan has just finished a path around the house, helped by someone called Mike. In front of the high window in the kitchen, a rockery is planted with shrubs. Grey wagtails perch on high thin branches of a young beech tree near the road, beside the natural hedge. Aidan decided not to remove it, when he began to build the house. He said this once, one Sunday in the Bog Road.

'He likes nature,' Barbara had said. 'So do I.'

Delia walks on the lawn. Aidan has planted shrubs and flowers along the drive. The sounds and smells are different in the Country. There are not many houses nearby. Cattle lew in the field. Delia is lost as she walks on the morning dew. The colours of the Country merge into a curtain, closing across her line of vision. Noises of crows and wind lifted branches grow into a crescendo. Delia feels like she will give birth, there is something inside her, growing. The embryo curled and uncurled within.

Now the curtain is gone and the colours resume their positions in the odd shaped garden. There is one shrub, Delia does not know its name, it has a deep purple colour. This colour stays out of proportion longer than the others. Yet eventually, it too shrinks back to its normal size, oozing into its template of a plant in the odd shaped garden in the Country.

There are different faces in the Country. Wrinkled faces, Delia does not recognise, but faces all the same, eyes, nose, mouth, voice somewhere around them, arms and legs. She walks into the post office holding her green pension book. People queue up for their weekly payment. Delia does not know any of the people there. Some of them nod to her, smiling, but most stare out the windows. Barbara waits outside in the motor car, looking in her beige handbag. Delia becomes accustomed to the sights and sounds of the Country. They become part of the daily routine. Mrs Freeley does not call anymore.

At first, Delia does not travel much in the Country. Other people, other places, other times, this must have been the time all along, this must have been the real time. The stability, the regularity, the people, the air, the smells, the different world. Soon she travels again. The other places come back and she is gone and they are shouting, they are asking her questions and they are nodding to each other and pouring a cup of tea. More tablets are handed to her. Green. Blue. Green and Blue. Red and Green. Green and Black. Black and Green. Green and Black.

'Yes indeed, Delia-well, that-is-what-I-said-to-Michael. We should have gotten the windows done years ago. But it's-hard-to-be paying for everything you know?' Delia sits between the square table and the pine presses against the wall in the kitchen in the house in the Country. She does not know the woman who speaks, sitting across from her at the square table. The woman's hair is tightly curled around her head which darts quickly around the room.

Delia lies in the bed, looking at the poster of the kitten on the ceiling. She stares at the poster for hours, the pink wool, the soft fabric of the pillow under the kitten's head, the small paw, sticking out over the top of the blanket. The kitten looks safe.

Delia hears a guitar. Aidan plays country songs, such as 'Bobby McGee' and 'Country Roads'. Aidan has a strong voice. It cuts through the walls between Delia's room and the kitchen in the house in the Country. Aidan brings her a cup of tea every night in between songs. Sometimes Aidan has visitors. Aidan boils the black plastic kettle and opens packets of biscuits. There is laughter and talk. When Barbara comes home later, they talk in the kitchen, but Delia cannot clearly hear what they are saying.

'Terrible prices,' Aidan says, one day he returns at noon. Delia stands at the sink, looking out the high window in the kitchen. The eye can see far in the Country, over many fields to the horizon. It is not like that in the Bog Road, there is only the unplastered block wall, the white back gate and James Meade's shed at the end of the garden. Here in the Country, Delia can see the roofs of houses and hay sheds in the distance.

'Sold for less than I bought, and that is after feeding them. I don't know, this farming carry-on,' Aidan is saying.

'Maybe we should go to Canada!' Barbara says.

'Canada?'

'Yeah. Rent out the land and just go, what do you think?'

'Yeah. Maybe. Maybe I'll get a brochure.'

Delia lies in the bed. She hears a noise somewhere in the house. Aidan is not playing the guitar. Delia looks around in the faint moonlight. She wonders has Thomas fallen over and hurt his head. James Meade is not in the bed beside her. Delia gets up and puts on her red slippers. She finds her cane walking stick at the chair with the compartment underneath for emergencies. She takes her faded green cardigan from the tall shiny teak wardrobe and slides it on. She opens the door, turning the brass doorknob, and looks down the long hall. The house is quiet. It is daytime. It is night-time. The dawn is coming. It is evening. It is morning. The house is quiet. This is not her house. This is another house. Somebody else's house. Delia does not know how she got to this house. Is this a house? She walks down the long hall, tapping her cane walking stick against the plain teak skirting board. She stops at the middle bedroom and opens the door. The light is on. Inside, a girl with black curly hair lies in bed, holding a teddy bear in her right arm. The girl's thumb is in her mouth. Her eyes are shut. Her cheeks are red. Delia looks around the room. It is painted pink. The curtains are not fully closed. There are dolls, toys, other teddy bears, drawings on light white paper scattered around the floor.

'Hello?' Delia says. The girl does not answer. Delia tuts. She turns and walks back into the long hall and down to the corner. She opens the next door. The light is on.

A baby lies in a cot, asleep, a soother in his mouth. Delia knows it is a boy because he is dressed in blue and boys are always dressed in blue. In the bed near the window an older boy lies. He has thick curly black hair. His eyes are open. He watches Delia.

'Hello,' Delia says.

'Hello gran,' the boy says.

'Do you know what time it opens?' Delia says.

'I- I don't know, gran,' the boy says.

Delia turns the corner to the front hall, where there is a tumble drier beside a small table which has a brown telephone on top.

There is a grunting noise. Delia gets nearer the front door. To one side is the door into the sitting room. To the right the door of Barbara and Aidan's room is ajar. The woman turns her head toward the door. She looks to be in her twenties.

Aidan looks up to the doorway. He jumps back, falling over his trousers on the ground, his buttocks rise in the air. He grabs a towel off the bed, wraps it around his waist. The bedroom door is shut with a bang.

'Are you alright, Delia?' Aidan says, his voice muffled.

'I heard a noise.'

'Ah, that's just the cattle outside.'

'Oh.'

'Go on to bed, Delia, good night.'

Delia walks back to her room at the other end of the house, tapping the cane walking stick against the plain teak skirting board.

Delia falls asleep and dreams of the brown patterned carpet, the Challen Evans miniature piano, the souvenir cups, one in a half-moon shape with 'You asked for a half cup of tea' printed on the outside, and another, the white plastic mug, with a split along the side and 'Tea Break' in cracked font stamped across it. She dreams of the red tiled mantelpiece, the tall window she used to look out to the sky, beyond the surreal shapes in the sheets as they lifted in the wind.

10.

Delia is in the Renault 12. Aidan taps the steering wheel as he drives. The village in the Country is not like the villages on the postcards in Kevin's shop. There is no main thoroughfare with church at one end and pub at the other. There is no neat terrace of houses with one window and a front door, windowsills painted a cheery colour.

Hawthorns and crabapple hedging line the roads. Bungalows are partly hidden from view. One streetlight stands over the forecourt of the combined village shop and post office. A half-mile from the shop is a local pub called Joyce's, a plain white building with narrow windows and a flat roof.

'That was old Johnny Long's workshop, there,' Aidan says, pointing to a barn. One galvanised sheet remains on the roof, the decaying rafters partly concealed by clumps of ivy.

'And over there beside Joyce's, was where my father used to sell lambs in the forties and fifties. It's all big marts now, less money for the small farmer,' Aidan says.

'The big shots have it all sewn up. Are we going for a pint, so?' Thomas says, looking out from the back seat, his cigarette clouding the motor car.

Delia turns her head around. 'When did you come?'

'Yesterday, Ma!' Thomas half-smiles at Delia, his stained white shirt is open at the top, vacant buttonholes partly concealed by clumps of curly grey chest hair. Delia notices another of Thomas' front teeth is missing.

'What happened your tooth, Joseph?'

'Oh yeah, I forgot to tell ye. I only have six left and one of them went wrong lately. I should have got them all out years ago when I was at it. Fucking driving me mad for the last month. Had to get the gate. I got the dentist in Ringsend to pull her Tuesday, a tenner, for twenty minutes, d'ya ever hear the likes!'

'Shush,' Delia says.

Joyce's has a long bar counter which runs the length of the building. Two men sit along it at either end on narrow high stools, their elbows rest on the laminated surface. A football match plays on the television in the corner. Aidan, Thomas and Delia sit at a round table near the window. Delia sips a sherry. Thomas slugs from a pint of Guinness. Aidan scratches his chin through his goatee as he swirls around the last mouthful of lager in the glass. 'What parish is this?' Delia says.

'It's a funny thing,' Aidan says. 'There are actually two parishes. This village is a postal area, you see.'

'Two parishes?' Delia says.

'Yes. Everyone across the road from us goes to the other church.'

'How did they manage that?' Thomas says.

'I suppose you have to split it somewhere.'

'In the middle of the village, though. Bleddy stupid,' Thomas says.

'Well, it's a postal area, you see.'

'No doubt it was the Brits set it up like that. That crowd! Pure awkward!'

'I think our post office was set up in the 20s.'

'And what do they do with the kids?' Delia says.

'Huh?'

'At communion? From this village, they don't all go to the one church?'

'A few goes to one and the rest to the other,' Aidan says. 'Our side is usually smaller. I was the only one from our school when I was making it.'

'You'd want your own church here,' Delia says.

'Maybe you're right, Delia,' Aidan says. 'They have a match between the two parishes down in the sports field every year.'

'I might have known the football would come into it,' Thomas says.

'Did you ever play, Tom?' Aidan says.

'A bit when I was young. No time though. Too busy working,' Thomas says, finishing his pint.

Delia gets up in the morning at eight o clock. The house is quiet. She wants to go to Mass but she cannot get to Mass during the week in the Country. She puts on her grey skirt and her faded grey jumper. She slides on her red slippers. She coughs. She takes her rosary beads from the half-moon table and sits on the chair with the compartment underneath for emergencies. She recites the Mysteries of the Rosary, passing the beads through her hands. She looks out through the chink of light between the curtains at the field where the cattle graze. She finishes the Mysteries and puts the rosary beads back on the half-moon table at the window. She takes her teeth from the jar of cloudy water, shakes them and fits them around her gums. She takes up her cane walking stick, turns the brass doorknob and opens the door. She walks down the long hall to the bathroom, tapping the walking stick against the skirting board. She washes her face with the carbolic soap on the sink, dries her skin with a flowery towel and straightens her hair with a thick handled brush. She walks up to the kitchen at the top of the house. There is no gas cooker in the house in the Country. The range is cold. She fills the black plastic kettle and plugs it in. She sits on the chair between the square table and the pine presses and looks out the high window over the sink. From the chair, all she can see is the grey sky. She sighs.

Aidan often bangs his head on the presses above the square table. 'I made them too low,' he says one day. Sometimes, somebody, Barbara, wants something from the press behind Delia's chair and Delia has to get up and they have to pull the chair out to get at the press. Barbara does not keep anything she needs very often in this press, however.

Aidan usually sits at the other side of the square table. His chair is up against the door into the dining room. Every time anyone wants to go in or out by this door, Aidan must get up. He moves his chair forward, but the door still hits the backrest. When Aidan gets up from his chair to go and do his herding every morning, he walks out of the kitchen into the odd shaped area they call the back hall. Here coats hang in a line along a short wall. This causes a problem when anyone comes from the long hall. The door into the long hall hits the coats on the short wall every time. There are too many coats on each hook and they fall and Aidan is often picking up the fallen coats. Aidan then puts on his wellingtons and somebody else, often Barbara, comes in from the long hall and, opening the door, bangs against Aidan's head.

Delia sits on the chair between the square table and the pine presses, listening to the succession of bangings, from the open pine press door over the square table which Aidan hits his forehead against, to the door into the dining room hitting against the backrest of Aidan's chair, usually this door is opened by the boy or the girl, and then the coats falling in the back hall and sometimes the door into the long hall being opened, often by Barbara, striking Aidan on the head while he puts on his wellingtons. Bang-bang-clunk-bang, bang-bang-clunk-bang, bang-bang-bang-bang, clunk-clunk-clunk, bang-bang-bang-bang, clunk-clunk-clunk. Bang.

Delia mooches around the house in the Country. She walks through the back hall, looking into the back toilet, the long hall, the first room where she sleeps, the girl's bedroom, the boys' bedroom, the front hall, the bathroom, the back toilet, Barbara and Aidan's bedroom, the sitting room and the dining room. She sits in the kitchen on the chair between the square table and the pine presses. 'What are you looking for, mammy?' Barbara says.

'Agnes.'

'What are you doing with that bottle?'

'I thought she'd call in. I wonder is she alright.'

'She—'

'I wonder will she be in today.'

'Mammy, Agnes died last year. You were at the funeral.'

'It's not like her not to call in during the week.'

Delia goes to Mass with Barbara, Aidan and the three children. They do not go every week. They go every so often. The grounds of the church are decorated with tall pine trees. Within, the Stations of the Cross are depicted on paintings smaller than in the town church. There are no marble pillars. The Country priest celebrates a quicker mass than the Town priest. He does not spend as long on the sermon. There are more local announcements in the Mass in the Country.

The first reading is done by the woman whom Delia saw in Barbara and Aidan's bedroom. The woman looks older. When she returns to her pew, she sits beside a man and two children. The second reading is done by someone called Mike. Aidan whispers that Mike is their next-door neighbour. Delia does not know who the man is that whispers to her. She does not know anybody here. She wants to go home now.

After Mass, Delia sits on a white deal chair in the sitting room near the arch into the dining room. Usually, visitors arrive on Sunday afternoon. Joseph comes every week with his wife Maureen and their daughter Maureen. Big Maureen is slightly smaller than Small Maureen but they were called Big and Small due to their ages and not their heights. Delia had always called them Big Maureen and Small Maureen since Small Maureen had been born.

They sit with Barbara's family amongst the mauve linen three-piece suite. Small Maureen always sits and never speaks. She perches on an armchair across from a beige plain concrete cast fireplace that

Aidan had fitted with someone called Mike. Barbara and Aidan sit on a three-seater settee against one wall. Sometimes the girl sits with them. The youngest child walks around the sitting room in a circle, falling over now and then, sucking on a soother, or sitting on the lilac carpet, playing with a train. The boy is rarely in the sitting room. Delia sometimes watches him in the odd shaped garden outside where he kicks a ball, talking to himself as he does. In the third armchair Joseph sits.

Big Maureen never sits and always speaks. 'There was a lot of them, too many of them, sure what could you, I said, I said to Joseph, we should go, no point...no point at all...of course...sure you know...oh yes we had to go...you couldn't...I said to Joseph and Maureen was in the shop, oh yes we had to go...oh yes it was time...sure you couldn't...no...you couldn't...there was too many...a lot of them, a way too many crazy...sure what could you do...do you know...do you know it was crazy a lot of them,' Big Maureen says.

Some Sundays, this party is joined by Mary, Margaret and Philly and the three Jacks and the three daughters of the three Jacks. The three daughters run around the odd shaped garden with the boy. There is a large crowd in the sitting room then and the three Jacks move out to the dining room, squeezing past Delia, they sit around a rectangular table, drinking Jameson and talking. 'They should all be ran out of England,' Jack is saying.

'They should,' Jack says.

'The whole lot of them, the whole fucking race of them,' Jack says.

'They should be shot,' Jack says.

'Now, now,' Aidan says.

'It says in the paper that they have taken over the place. It's no wonder there's no work there for Paddy. Fucking crowd.'

'What they need to do is take them all out and shoot them. Have you more whiskey there, pet?'

'I think you've had enough.'

'It's the only way, sure the mothers are having the kids and the kids are growing up like the fathers, wasters, trouble-makers. Shoot them all, that's what they should do, definitely. Get rid of them. Fucking multiplying like rabbits, they are.'

'Where did you get the sandals?'

'Heaton's, they were reduced. I hope she doesn't grow out of them before the winter.'

During these large meetings, Delia sometimes moves out to the kitchen, where she sits, her hands on the surface of the square table and she looks out the high window at the grey sky.

The Bog Road is a long way from the Country. Delia does not know how long. She does not know how she would get back to the Bog Road.

'Maurice says the bathroom roof needs to be done,' Barbara says to Aidan. He eats a slice of toast at the square table. Delia washes a plate in the sink in the kitchen. She looks across at the first pine press. Its door is open directly over Aidan. Aidan will bang his forehead against it when he stands up as he does most days. Within, on the top shelf are the two souvenir cups that Kathleen had brought home from Watford and Delia had hung under the shelf over the cooker in the back kitchen in the house in the Bog Road, with 'You Asked for Half a Cup of Tea' on one and 'Tea Break' on the other. They were in the back kitchen in the house in the Bog Road and now they are in the press above Aidan's head in the kitchen in the house in the Country.

Thump-thump, thump-thump-thump, thump-thump, thump-thump-thump is the noise every night outside Delia's room in the house in the Country. Thump-thump, thump-thump-thump, thump-thump, thump-thump-thump. Delia does not know what the noise is. She asks Barbara but Barbara does not seem to hear her. She asks others in the house. They do not seem to hear her either. The noise keeps her awake. It seems like a gunshot, on the path outside, like they have on the television in the sitting room. Delia lies in the darkness, her eyes open, phlegm catching the air as it travels up and down the windpipe and she coughs. Cough-cough, cough-cough-cough. Thump-thump. Cough-cough-cough. Thump-thump, thump-thump-thump. There is silence. Cough-cough. Cough-cough-cough. Thump-thump, thump-thump-thump. Cough.

Mrs Freeley does not visit anymore. Delia sits at the square table in the kitchen in the house in the Country and looks out the high window at the grey sky. She wipes the surface of the square table with a green cloth. There is no cigarette smoke from Mrs Freeley. The curly-haired woman, a Mrs Somebody, comes every few days and talks to Barbara.

'How-are-you, and how-is-yourself,' Mrs Somebody says.

'Hello, Aine,' Barbara says, when Mrs Somebody comes. The boy stands in the kitchen with a mouth organ.

'Do you want to hear a tune?' the boy says. He brings the mouth organ to his lips and begins to play. Delia does not like the sound. She nods at the boy. Mrs Somebody snorts and the boy stops playing and leaves the kitchen.

'And how is Jackie?' Barbara says.

The people in the kitchen drift around as though on a skating rink, like the surface of the Bog Road when a freezing night follows rain and the children skate, singing and whooping and shouting and yelping. It is like that now in the kitchen in the house in the Country, the people around Delia are sliding, their borders merge together and Delia is skating too, she is holding onto Maisie and they are screaming with joy as they career toward a wall and manage to swing themselves away from it just in time. The figures in the kitchen in the house in the Country blend until they are blue and green, fragments sliding into the fading black background. Delia sighs.

Delia lies in the bed. There is a smell of perfume. A child cries as a hairbrush is trawled through a scalp.

'We are going to Mass, mammy,' Barbara says, as she looks into the room. They do not bring Delia to Mass anymore. The birch front door closes and the house in the Country is silent. The tall shiny teak wardrobe, from the back room in the house in the Bog Road, leans forward as though the floor underneath is off level. If it fell, it would land upon her. She looks down at her arms in the wide folds of her nightdress. She is thinner now. A collection of bones and veins and organs, and the tall shiny teak wardrobe would crush her. She coughs. The phlegm is still stuck in her throat.

'Will you bring the children in and count them?' Delia says.

In the odd shaped back hall, Delia pours milk over jellied rabbit and chicken liver in a steel bowl. She opens the back door and a black and white collie rushes in, his jaws around the meat, sucking, slurping, chewing, his belly rippling.

Delia pads through the long hall, tapping her cane walking stick against the skirting board ahead of her, turning the corner to where the tumble drier whirrs, a belt buckle hanging off a pair of trousers crashes against the drum inside. She comes to the door of the sitting room and mooches in. She looks out the window, over the drive, beyond the purple shrub at the stone wall, across the road beyond and out into the horizon. She can see the mountain near the coast. The day is clear, she can find the path, curving as it inclines up the mountain.

Now she walks the path with Maisie, holding hands, reaching the statue of St Patrick and looking at pilgrims, kneeling and circling it seven times. Others go past in bare feet, mumbling, chanting a hymn as they climb. On a stone stile outside the pub on the road, at the foot of the mountain, Delia shares an apple with Maisie, looking at the hawkers, standing at their shaky wooden tables, selling stout climbing sticks and glass bottles of fizzy pop.

Delia lies in the darkness. There is jagged conversation in the kitchen in the house in the Country. 'No, nothing…'

'Why, why?' Barbara says.

'Why?' again.

'Please.' This is Aidan speaking now.

Moaning, whining, moaning, shouting, screaming, moaning, whining. Kissing.

For months and years, Delia mooches around the house in the Country, folding towels that were already folded, sweeping floors that were already swept, wiping tables that were already wiped. The cane walking stick is not enough, now she has two, now she has a Zimmer frame. Arms help her up, help her down, help her in, help her out. She stopped going out to the road to hitch a lift to the Bog Road after the first year in the Country. She does not go outside anymore. The house in the Bog Road is a dream, it is gone, it never was or it never will be again.

Delia's coughing circles through the house all night. It is a straining, useless effort at removing the phlegm from cavities in the larynx. Every morning, she ends the night's coughing with an almighty effort of breath. Aidan comes with a cup of tea. He takes the faded grey skirt from the bottom of the tall shiny teak wardrobe. He helps Delia take off her night dress and put on the skirt. He guides her to the Zimmer frame. 'When do you think I could go home, Michael?' Delia says.

'Soon, now Delia, soon.' Aidan says, scratching his beard. His goatee has grown out, his jaw is now hidden underneath dense clumps of black curly hair. He can no longer reach his jaw with his fingers.

It is evening. There are low tones coming through Delia's door. 'Here…there…needs a few quid…he…across…oh…right…'
Delia cannot hear properly.

Someone visits often now. The same associated sounds, voice, smacking of lips, cleaning of pipe, rattling of tobacco paper. One day she meets the visitor, a thin man with a grey suit, who walks stooped over.

'Hello, Delia,' the man says. 'And how are you getting on? I moved the bird repeller to the other side of the potato field, sorry if twas keeping ye awake,' the man says to the room in general.

'Not at all, Mike, we never heard it did we, Aidan?' Barbara says.

'No,' Aidan says, scratching his beard.

Mike's pipe is a little like James Meade's, only it has more of a twist on it. Other evenings, when Delia is in bed in the room, Mike comes and talks in low tones and Barbara and Aidan talk in low tones as well, as if that is their way, which it has not been before. Sometimes, the back door opens and Mrs Somebody comes in and the tones change to quicker and louder and more broken, and people vie for attention. Then, after a couple of hours, Mrs Somebody leaves and the tones revert to low and paced and there are more pauses.

The back door closes. 'Says he will be able to pay us back.'

The boy opens the door in the room where Delia lies in the bed. There is a smell of Sudo cream in the room. Delia opens her eyes. The boy has thick curly black hair and large green eyes. He has black eyebrows which are close to joining, they make a faint 'v' over his nose. He walks in toward the bed, holding a mug of milky tea in his left hand. In his right hand, he holds two digestive biscuits. 'Hi gran,' he says. 'Cup of tea and a few biscuits?'

The boy dips the biscuit in the tea for too long and part of it comes away and floats in the tea. He dips some of the remainder for less time. He offers the dipped end to Delia, whose eyes are closed.

The boy tries to force the biscuit in between Delia's lips. It breaks against her gums. Pieces fall onto the front of her throat which lies out beyond her chin. Delia's eyes open. She looks to her right. The boy's eyes widen. His mouth makes an 'o'. Delia sticks her tongue out, wrapping it around the piece of biscuit, pulling it into her mouth, lifting her tongue over the grey hairs above her upper lip, clearing away the remainder of the biscuit debris. The boy brings the mug of tea to her lips. Delia fits her lips around the rim and sucks in the tea. She swallows and smiles.

The boy gives Delia part of the second biscuit, also dipped for a shorter period of time. She opens her mouth and takes in part of the biscuit. Her gums crush the soft mush soundlessly and she swallows it. She smiles and coughs.

The boy offers in the mug and Delia's fingers softly take the handle and she pours the rest of the tea down her throat.

The boy reaches in and kisses Delia on the lips, her grey hairs bristle against his smooth skin. The boy shivers and draws back.

'See you later gran,' he says, walking to the door, carrying the empty cup.

11.

Delia can hear voices. They are real voices. They are not voices from another time. They sound clear. They are familiar. It is like they are in the front room of the house in the Bog Road, but that cannot be. Delia stares at the poster on the ceiling of the kitten under the pink blanket. 'Tis terrible, now,' one of the Jacks was saying.

'Tis, tis,' another one says.

'We should have done away with this crowd,' a third Jack says.

'Are we going down for one?' Thomas says.

'Yeah, sure,' Aidan says.

'We have to be going home,' Joseph says.

Delia does not go into the sitting room on Sunday afternoons anymore. She stays mostly in her room now. Here, she eats a mashed bowl of cornflakes in the morning, a mashed bowl of potatoes at lunch, a mashed bowl of beans in the evening. Drips of soft food stick to her bib throughout the day.

In the sitting room everyone drinks tea or whiskey and eats fruit cake and sandwiches or smokes cigarettes. There are footsteps and talk, muffled unknown words, unknown sounds, doors opening, doors closing. Joseph comes into the room and sits on the chair with the compartment underneath for emergencies.

'Hello, mammy,' Joseph says.

'Is that you, Jim?' Delia says.

'No, mammy, it's Joseph.'

'Are you from the midlands as well?'

'How are you getting on now in the Country, mammy? Do you like it here?'

'Where are you from in the midlands?'

'Maureen and little Mo send their regards, mammy.'

'Jimmy was from the midlands but he came west. How much do I owe you?

'I better be going. I'll see you soon, mammy.'

Joseph kisses Delia on the lips. His thick moustache prickles against her skin. He leaves the room, closing the door behind him.

Delia lies awake in the bed in the room in the house in the Country. The boy sits on the chair with the compartment underneath. He plays with a train. He runs the train along the aluminium armrests off the end, where he suspends it as though travelling on an imaginary track in midair.

'We are going to the Bog Road now,' Aidan says, looking in the doorway. 'We will only be an hour or so. We just have to measure the bathroom.'

Delia is unable to move her legs, unable to move her arms. She stares at the poster of the kitten on the ceiling. The paw sticks out over the top of the pink blanket. Delia is closing her eyes. 'Hail Mary full of grace…' Delia says in the empty room, her voice seems out of place. 'The Lord is with thee, blessed art thou amongst women and blessed is the fruit of thy womb…'

A cold piece of digestive biscuit is stuck to a hair on her chin. She tries to remove it with her tongue. The mush has hardened in the air. She cannot move it.

It is 1946. Delia is forty-two years old. Barbara is a small baby in her arms, in her arms, growing up into a girl, into a teenager, into a woman, into a woman, she is a child, Delia is a child, lost somewhere, grabbing for the wall, nothing beside her, no wall there, no floor underneath. She looks around for the front door of the house in the Bog Road. There is no door, there is no Bog Road, there is no room, there is no Country, she gasps.

'There is a ration on this, woman,' James Meade says, holding the half-empty packet of sugar in the back kitchen in the house in the Bog Road. 'Bleddy ridiculous, we are not even involved in this bleddy war,' James Meade says.

'Shush, that's terrible language for a man from the Royal County,' Delia says.

'It's no wonder in this bleddy place,' James Meade says.

Noise in the room, noise in the sitting room, in the house, in the Country, noise in Delia's head now, noise all over the house, noise all over the noise, and she lies back, looking up at the ceiling, still trying to remove the piece of biscuit, still trying, still trying. Then she stops.

Aidan comes into the room on a Saturday afternoon. He smiles at Delia. The boy comes in behind him.

'Want to watch a bit of telly, Delia?' Aidan says. 'You bring the blanket,' he tells the boy. Aidan takes the plastic beaker off the bed and places it on the half-moon table. He unties Delia's bib. Dried mush falls in a haze of crumbs. He slowly pulls the blankets back. He wraps his arm around Delia's body and lifts her up from the bed and carries her out through the long hall, the odd shaped back hall, the kitchen and into the dining room, where now there is a two-seater couch across the arch and a Grundig television. Barbara is keeping the sitting room good for visitors.

Delia lies on the couch, wrapped in a blanket. She cannot move her legs. There is just a curtain of flesh flapping underneath her bones. The boy comes into the dining room carrying two digestive biscuits and a beaker of tea. Delia tries to keep her eyes open. There are flashing images on the television, noises, she watches swallows pass through the sky, it must be autumn, they are migrating, Delia wants to migrate, to return, to come home, to go home.

The boy sits on the floor, his knees tucked underneath him, in the same position as Delia. Delia feels pain. She coughs and coughs and coughs and coughs. The phlegm is stuck in the cavities of her wind-pipe and breaks up the flow of air.

'Where is Thomas?' Delia says.

'I don't know, gran,' the boy says.

'When am I going home, laddin'?' Delia says.

'I don't know, gran,' the boy says.

Delia has separated, her legs are ahead of her, her arms are behind her, her torso is beyond her. She lies back on the bed. Aidan is gone. The television is gone. The poster is still above her head, the items are still on the half-moon table at the window. The Mickey Mouse wallpaper is still on the wall across from her, beside the recessed space, where the tall shiny teak wardrobe from the back room in the house in the Bog Road still stands off level.

Delia is a child running through grass as fast as she can, her cheeks are hot, her vision blurring with the air running into her face, she laughs in the cardiac buzz.

'Wait, Dee, wait!' Maisie says from behind her. Delia's legs are short and bony, she chews a piece of apple she found in an orchard. They run through the grass, which is up past their waists.

'Get ourra me meadow!' a man says. It is not her father, it is their neighbour, the neighbour in a house near the sea. The boy sits, beside the bed, on the chair with the compartment underneath for emergen-cies. Delia is at the carnival with her friends and James Meade, they are all talking, Delia cannot hear the words, only the noise, the noise continues. Delia lies in the bed, trying to eat the piece of biscuit the boy is pushing into her mouth. She wants to go home now.

'When am I going home?' Delia says.

'I don't know, gran,' the boy says.

Delia lies in the bed, there are noises outside the window. A gust of wind blows around the house. Delia's breath catches on the mounds of phlegm in her larynx like turbulence. Delia moves a little as she breathes in and out. Her mouth is half-open. Her fingers grip the top of the blanket as though to stop anyone suddenly pulling it away from her. A car drives along the country road. It is cloudy.

The boy sits still. He cannot leave the room. Granny might stop breathing. Granny might die. He watches her body inhale and exhale, slowly struggling. He is there to keep Delia company. Delia's eyes open and close every few minutes. She lifts her hand at one stage, and then lets it drop.

Delia is thinner now, thinner than even the defined frame she carried a few months earlier. The boy's eyes search Delia for signs of recovery, improvement, a return to health, but there is none. He takes a train from his right-hand jacket pocket and drives it along the aluminium armrest of the chair with the compartment underneath. Now to one side, now to the other and then until the train runs off the end and he lets it go and it falls to the beige linoleum below, making a clack as it lands. Delia stirs in her half sleep.

In the bed, Delia dreams of things gone by. Mixtures of things, concoctions of people and places, swirling together, country and town, here and there, now and then, becoming a swaying mass, an oozing gluey lump of fat as though in a gigantic frying-pan, or melting on a piece of steel, floating in an abyss, in the universe, somewhere, people who never existed created from the stains of others, joining together and separating, Delia travels quickly through the stars and the darkness like a zooming meteorite, into the primordial ooze of a world, lost in the bizarre, in the cycle of creation and regeneration, the thick lost fabrics of man and woman, hopelessly lost and now, she does not understand and cannot understand, and tries to remember, tries to remember all, but she cannot, she never can, trying to recreate words and phrases and times and people and actions and it all becomes a confusing jungle of things, a dazzling mishmash of unknowable objects, a grim matrix of fear and uncertainty and she lies there breathing poorly, her body unmoving, her time spent and not spent.

There are hundreds of voices, thousands of voices speaking to Delia in her mind, outside her mind, she cannot see the voices, she is afraid, she looks, but cannot see, all that is there is the poster of the kitten tucked under the blanket and yet the noise gets louder and louder, booming, laughter, crying and shouting, whispering, all types of tones and accents speaking as one. A huge tangle, Delia is bothered and confused, her mind feels like the mane of a girl's hair in the morning, full of knots, and she had a hairbrush and is trying to untangle the convolutions, but it is useless, unlike the hair which eventually straightens, these knots never resolve themselves, only tightening more and more, refusing to conform, refusing to be controlled, tangling and knotting even more all the time, more and more, and Delia is tired.

Aidan opens the door. 'Granny is asleep, is she?' he says.

Delia is not dead, not yet. The boy sits in her room every day, playing with his train, looking at her chest go up and down, her body shuddering. He feeds her a beaker of tea and digestive biscuits some days, not every day, some days he does this.

The boy nods at Aidan and runs out of the room and down the long hall and through the front hall and out the front door and runs around into the odd shaped garden kicking his ball, and Delia goes into a deep sleep.

'Cost...cost...I wonder...' Delia lies in the dark. Muffled words come through the block wall.

'Tax rebate...yeah...yeah...yeah...'

'He was saying...down in Joyce's...'

'Yeah...yeah...yeah...'

'That's interesting...' Aidan says.

Delia stares in the darkness clutching the blankct. There is still some moisture on her chin from the milk she had with her mush an hour earlier. She hears the guitar.

'Busted flat near Baton Rouge...' Aidan's voice comes through. He has a good singing voice, very good, good on the guitar too. Delia's mind follows the tune of the song, up and down the chords and pauses and repeats and onwards, up and down her mind follows it, her eyes blink, she hears other music somewhere, not sure where, somewhere in the distance, distant music, distant songs, distant people. Here is the noise of youth, a violin playing at the fair on a cold Saturday morning. Coppers in the hat in front of the musician.

Cattle lew at Delia, their huge eyes blink, froth drips from their mouths. Her and Maisie swing from their father's waist, their free arms waving from flowery dresses over up-turned green wellingtons. 'Howya Tom!'

'How are ye, men? Did ye sell?'

'Kirby did. Prices are up. Did ye bring a lock of ewes, it's the day for selling?'

'No, I'm buying a few weather hoggets. I'll fatten them and butcher next back-end.'

'Oh, aye. The hogget sale hasn't started yet.'

'Look at the ponies!' Maisie says, jumping a little. Two Shetland foals stare at Delia from behind a wooden gate. The gate is worn smooth from hides rubbing against the corner. The long elegant heads look aloof of the cattle around them.

'Aye, a real pair of beauts,' Delia's father says. 'Come on, I have things to do.'

In the field a group of men talk in a corner. 'Hie Tom, how were the hoggets? Did you buy yet?' The group laugh.

'Daddy, that man is talking to you,' Maisie says.

'Come on, we have to go,' Delia's father says, pulling their arms forward as they walk away. The men's guffaws follow them and mix with bleating sheep and lowing cattle and braying donkeys and gates closing and banging and there is a smell of dung.

Someone spits on the ground, the saliva sticks to the loose clay, rolls into a ball, bringing the specks of dust around attached to it, picking up other debris on the way, nothing more than a distilled ball of juice from a wide mouth. Laughs of men echoing, long dead, gone to worms, to maggots, rotted away in graveyards, to dust and Delia lies in the bed in the room in the house in the Country, thinking of those men, of hats and wide trousers and windy sticks and hob-nailed boots and laughter and pipe smoke and thick fingers gripping a roll of notes after the sales at eleven o'clock.

12

In the odd shaped garden, the boy runs around kicking the ball ahead of him, running to it, kicking it against a two-foot bank near the hedge along the road. Four shrubs planted by Aidan are used as goal-posts. Across the lawn runs a narrow slope which makes the pitch off level. The boy plays around a large rock in the corner unearthed during building excavations, where he sometimes leaves his jumper if he gets too hot. He kicks the ball up, high, watching it fall, bouncing against the two electric cables which pass over the garden. They are the reason he cannot fly a kite. He wanted to fly a kite in the garden but he cannot because it is too dangerous. If he wants to fly a kite, he must go into the field and the ground is very soft there and there is dung. He does not want to go out into the field. Things are different out there. He likes the odd-shaped garden, he likes running around his own pitch.

When the ball bounces back, he traps it and dribbles, weaving in and out, in and out and then kicking it hard. The noise of words, the queue of sentences form in his head as he runs, his face burning, his cheeks a dark red and he speaks alone.

The boy moves from one player to another. Perfect names come to him to attach to them: Raker, Kiosk, Saper, Shanz. They are almost always called Jack. Jack Raker, Jack Kiosk, Jack Saper, Jack Shanz, what a fantastic player he is. The boy likes the name Jack, he doesn't like his own name.

These are great players, they are leaders, captains of the teams he plays against. He is captain of his team, he scores a wonderful goal in every match, where he gets the ball off his team's goalkeeper and dribbles past every player and when he gets to the other end, such is his genius, he mesmerises the other goalkeeper, now leaning one way, now leaning the other, before with a feint of such phenomenal trickery that the goalkeeper is dazzled and the boy simply side foots the ball into the net. Goal!!!!!!!

Jack Shanz is foreign. From which country the boy is not quite sure yet. When he writes up the report of the match in his 'newspaper' later in the evening, while Barbara is at work and Aidan is playing the guitar and before he brings Delia her evening beaker of tea and two digestive biscuits, he will write the name 'Shanz' and he will insert a strange symbol, a sideways 's' with a dot nesting in each curve. He invented this, this is not a language accent as far as he knows, but it lends a certain authenticity to the name, a sharper edge of believability, in his mind, in his match in the pitch, in the stadium, in the odd-shaped garden, outside the house, in the Country. Jack Kiosk is big and tough. Jack Saper is slight and skilful. But Shanz is magnificent, Shanz is a masterful controller of the ball. 'Masterful.'

'He is masterful, that lad,' Aidan says about one of the others in the boy's class. He scratches his beard. 'Elegant on the ball. Born with it.'

The boy thinks about this word, 'elegant,' as he runs around with the ball in the odd-shaped garden. He wonders how someone becomes 'elegant' and 'masterful' at football, how someone could achieve the status as described in the kitchen. He tries to control the ball 'elegantly', he tries to pass the ball 'elegantly', he tries to dribble with the ball 'elegantly'. He tries to imagine what is 'elegant' about being good at football? He does enjoy being what he imagines as 'elegant' but there is something not satisfying about it. Yet he can control the ball completely, here in the pitch, in the odd-shaped garden, alone.

At the school, the football matches he plays with the other boys are different to those he enjoys in the odd-shaped garden. He is always one of the last picked on teams, rarely gets the ball, never dribbles like he does in the odd-shaped garden, never makes resounding passes, 'resounding', that is one of the words his persona as the commentator uses, he has a name too, he calls him Pete Popse.

The boy does not involve his siblings in these games. They are too young. He wishes he could get them to play. Later, he will put one of them in goal while he plays his match outfield.

Delia slaps the boy on the hand as he gives her a digestive biscuit in the evening, in the winter, in her room, in the house in the Country, trying to do things she hasn't the strength to do anymore. The slap is not struck with any force, but her fingernail catches on his skin and cuts it, causing it to bleed.

The boy is mad. He wants to punch Delia hard, in the face, to hear the bone break. But he does not want to do this, he jumps back, he holds his breath, he exhales, his eyes are watering.

'Gimme it!' Delia says. Her nails are too long, the boy thinks, he wants to say: 'Don't hit me like that, gran.' But he does not, cannot, will not, cannot. He is three years old, Molly rubs his back, Delia smiles, he sits on a potty, he has his shorts down, he wants to pee, he does not want to pee, he runs around the front kitchen of the house in the Bog Road, wanting to pee, not wanting to pee, he cannot pee anywhere, the nappy is not there, he will wet the carpet, he must hold it, he must hold it now.

The boy brings the rest of the biscuit to a drawer in a square chest in his bedroom. It is full of 'newspapers', centrefolds from exercise books written in black or blue biro, margins drawn along the top and down the centre with a shatter-proof ruler. Headlines refer to televised football matches, Aidan's current farming jobs, household cleaning achievements. The mastheads include 'The Relator', 'The Morning Post', 'The Bugle.' The lettering is embellished with heavy inked fillings. The drawer is full. There is no room for biscuits, yet he pushes it in on top of the 'newspapers' and closes the drawer. He will not give Delia any more of the biscuit.

The boy sits on his bed. Scattered around the bedroom are cardboard boxes and drawers from dumped chests full of more 'newspapers' and 'magazines'. Mixed in are schoolbooks and diaries. Beside the bed is a green glass-topped locker packed with 'comics' and 'booklets' the boy has made, many made a long time ago, everything was made a long time ago.

Outside the door, at the corner of the long hall is a yellow trunk with the name 'Molly Meade' written on the bottom right-hand corner. The boy has written 'Toybox' across one of the panels. A small piece of yellowed paper with the words 'under-garments' is sellotaped across the top edge. The trunk is full of jumpers.

Now the boy sits on the chair with the compartment underneath, beside Delia's bed in her room, in the house, in the Country. He grips the aluminium armrests of the chair. Delia is sleeping. The boy stares at her, her eyelids flicker. The outside blends together exuding light and dark into the room and it all melts into a quivering heap of blues, blacks and greens and swirls and melts and he is lost, lost within the mix with Delia who is already lost, lost they are together now, swivelling down the hole in the ground.

Delia's chest heaves, she coughs, she splutters, the world is together, the world is broken, smashed to fragments and melted and poured back into a mould without all of the pieces, so the new piece is missing some of the original and the boy stares at the ceiling and the comfortable position of the kitten underneath the blanket, with one paw over the top.

The boy wants to go outside and run around the pitch in the stadium in the odd-shaped garden with his ball and play with Jack Shanz and Jack Saper and Jack Raker and Jack Kiosk and the others, including one player called Pete Bannister, commentated on by Pete Popse who is live at the stadium.

Barbara and Aidan go out at night sometimes. There is perfume in the air. Delia hears them leave through the front door, the clunk of the birch against its frame has become familiar over the years in the Country. A diesel engine starts, revving, drives away, chugging down the road.

There is something familiar about these noises now, in the house in the Country, something re-assuring about clunks and thumps and bangs. An argument between the children, the collie barking, a door closing, a gust of wind, the hum of a passing car. She is not alone when she hears these noises. She and the noises are together in the place, wherever it is, whatever it is. She may be dead, she does not know, cannot know. She lies in the dark. She tries to think, but it is hard, it is wearing, it is easier to lie and listen to the noises out there, somewhere. The noises are like a concrete wall, something to lean against, something to anchor against. What is difficult is the silence, the lack of noise, when the children go to bed and there is no noise in the house in the Country and Barbara and Aidan have not yet returned and there is no light and there is no noise. Now the humming of the boy comes through the long hall.

'Aaaah…aahhhaahhaahh…hahahah…aahh…aaah…aahhhaah haahh…hahahah…aahhhaaa…aahhaahhaahh…hahahah…hahahahah ahahah…aaahhhhaaaa…huhhahhuhhhhhh.'

There is a moving sound as though a bed is being jumped on. The chanting continues to come through the walls. Delia likes to hear this noise. It gives her comfort.

Delia sees a boy of thirteen or fourteen, his eyes wide, his hair dangling around his shoulders, his frame thin. 'How much do I owe you?' Delia says, looking around for her purse on the bed. The boy sits on the chair with the compartment underneath.

'Hi gran,' he says.

A procession of boys and men go through the room: James Meade, Thomas, boys from the coast, boys from the town, walking boys, running boys, lost boys, found boys, all types of boys, but this is not a boy, Delia thinks, this is somebody growing, growing up, not a boy now, becoming a man, but looking lost, Delia wants to take his hand and bring him somewhere, she does not know where, where to bring the boy, but he seems lost and she does too, together they may find a way out of the room in the house in the Country, together they will find a way, Delia smiles.

Delia looks at her fingers and catches her breath. Whose are these hands, whose is this body? The skin, marked with brown pocks, the veins coming through, black long snake-like channels rising along her limbs, arms like rods, with sagging flesh hanging off, who is this? How many children are there in the room in the house in the Country, someone needs to count the children, to bring them in and make sure they are all there and not at the lake or outside in their pyjamas in the depths of winter like poor Anthony, poor, poor Anthony and poor James Meade who went down to the grave every morning, poor, poor James. Poor people, poor, poor people. Delia wants to suck something, she pulls her hand up somehow to her mouth and puts her thumb in between her lips, closes her mouth and sucks.

The boy has gone. There is noise. Outside, a diesel engine dies. The front door opens. There are voices. Footsteps, the click of the black plastic kettle, the toaster primed. '...in great form.'

'Lost weight, she has...'

Toast buttered, cups are filled. 'Who was the man with the green jacket?'

There is noise in a bedroom. Shuffling. Panting. Springs. Whining. Then silence. Someone urinates in the bathroom. Then silence. Delia coughs in the darkness. Her arm stretches toward the half-moon table where there is a beaker of water. Her fingers hit the side of the beaker. She reaches again but cannot grasp it. She drops her arm and it falls, swinging gently at the side of the bed.

'Hello, Delia, how are you, how is the family?' Dr Crabbe says, swinging around on his chair, closing a drawer, as Delia enters the examination room.

'Not too bad, Doctor.'

'Great! How old is the last child now?'

'Philomena is seven.'

'Seven! Great! Yourself and Jim could do with a break from the babies, huh!'

'Yes, indeed Doctor.'

'So what can I do?'

'I've been very sick in the stomach the last month, you know...'

'Oh, yes, yes. Let's see...'

Dr Crabbe examines Delia. He puts a round disc on her chest, looks in her ears and eyes, tightens something on her arm. His hands are warm on her stomach.

'Hmm. There is something there, Delia. I'll arrange a scan for you but it will take a bit of time, the way things are in the hospitals at the moment.'

'What is it, Doctor?'

'Ah, these politicians, they don't know whether they are coming or–'

'No, I mean in my stomach?'

'Oh. We won't know until we get the scan done, Delia.'

'When will I get it, do you think?'

'Uh, it might take a while, a few weeks I'd say. Don't worry.'

'But would I not want to get seen to fairly soon?'

Dr Crabbe stares at Delia. 'Right, right. I'll set up a meeting with Mr Strachan in the hospital as well. He'll see you sooner than the scan. Maybe in the meantime...' Dr Crabbe opens a drawer. He shuffles around for a few moments, before producing a small container of pink tablets. 'These are not available here yet. They are Koch Antitoxins, my brother, you know Tony?'

'Oh, yes.'

'Yeah, he's a pharmacist in Boston. Take one of these every day. They'll help with the discomfort.'

Delia takes one of the pink tablets every morning. She did feel somewhat better. She does not say anything to James Meade about her illness. He has a lot on his mind. He leaves the house in the Bog Road every morning at half past seven. After Mass, he goes to the graveyard, and sits at Anthony's grave. He arrives home at between nine and half past. He sits at the round table, smoking a cigarette with the newspaper opened in front of him in the front kitchen in the house in the Bog Road. He looks out the tall window into the yard over the washing line toward the sky, his one functioning eye flickering, the blue around the pupil still clear, the other eye a dull white and blue lump of marble.

Delia takes the pink tablets for four weeks. A letter arrives. An appointment has been arranged at the hospital with a Mr Strachan.

On the day, Delia sets off, carrying her blue canvas bag in her right hand, having told James Meade that there was a sale in the butchers down the town. The hospital is crowded. People sit around on steel backed chairs in the entrance hall. A woman at a desk holds brown folders and looks through piles of paper sheets.

'Mr Strachan, was it?' the woman says.

Mr Strachan is a younger man than Dr Crabbe. He smiles and leads Delia to an examination bed in his office. 'Please lie here, Delia and open the bottom three buttons on your blouse,' Mr Strachan says. 'I've looked at Dr Crabbe's report and I want to do a preliminary examination.' Mr Strachan goes to his desk, as Delia gets on the bed, opening the bottom three buttons of her blouse and lying back on the thin pillow. Mr Strachan comes back and puts the round disc of his stethoscope on Delia's stomach. He nods at Delia and leaves the room. Delia lies still.

A nurse comes in a few minutes later. She puts her hands on Delia's stomach. Her hands are cold. 'You can sit up now and close your blouse, Delia,' the nurse says. She sits at Mr Strachan's desk and looks through a folder.

'What did Dr Crabbe tell you?'

'He said there was something there.'

Delia sits on the edge of the examination bed. The nurse looks across. 'I see,' the nurse says. 'There is something there. You are pregnant.' Delia moves on the examination bed.

'Dr Crabbe gave you–' the nurse looks at the folder on Mr Strachan's desk, 'Koch antitoxins. They are not regulated here, he must have gotten them in America.'

'He did.'

'They are used for ectopic pregnancies and temporary control of tumours. They are fine for adults but they are dangerous for a foetus.'

'He told me to take them.'

'I know that, Delia. We'll arrange a scan to see how the baby is, but there is a heartbeat so he or she is alive.'

Delia leaves the hospital through the crowded entrance hall. She walks down the street, back to the house on the Bog Road, her empty blue canvas bag gently rocking on her arm, her eyes fixed on the path ahead of her.

The family is very excited about the new baby. Delia and James Meade had not expected to have any more children after Philly.

Philly pushes a pram carrying Barbara along the path on the Bog Road. Barbara is a doll for her sisters. They get to dress her and feed her and change her and sing to her and tell her stories.

Barbara has a club foot and a purple birthmark on her left cheek. She walks with a hump on her back. Delia rocks Barbara in her arms every night in the front kitchen. James Meade stops going to Anthony's grave every morning. When he comes back from the church he puts Barbara on his knees and tells her of the seas and the countries and the governments and the sky and Heaven and hell and God and the Holy Spirit and the devil. At night, Delia tucks Barbara into her little bed in the front bedroom, singing her a lullaby and promising her nothing will ever harm her, not ever again.

It is a cold day outside. Donie and Sam are playing cards in the front room. Some of the girls are upstairs in the back room, smoking and talking, laughing about boys. Delia sits, knitting, on her armchair at the red tiled mantelpiece in the front kitchen. On the Grunow, a horn-pipe reel plays called 'Hand me down the tackle.' It is a tune Delia hears often, she likes it. Barbara sits at the round table drawing pictures in an exercise book. A doll lies beside some crayons. James Meade sits at the tall window, reading the paper. 'More cut-backs!' he says.

The black front gate is kicked open and Thomas walks down the path, his forehead glistens with sweat, his shirt is completely open, a cloud of stubble hangs around his jaw. One hand is anchored to his pocket. He stands in front of the red tiled mantelpiece, still, as though he had turned to stone.

Thomas returns to the house in the Bog Road every so often after he moved out. Usually at Easter or Christmas. He got married in 1950. He had been legally separated from his wife and child in 1953. Now he comes to the house, sometimes red-faced, sometimes with his shirt open, shouting about 'Bollockses in Dublin,' and 'Bastards in Manchester,' and 'Pricks in London.'

Thomas reaches over the black hearth, takes the poker off the hook within the red tiles and pokes the smouldering fire. 'What kind of a fire is that?' Thomas says. 'Arrah! Half a job!'

He flings the poker on the hearth, cracking one of the black tiles. Barbara runs upstairs with her doll.

'Why don't you hook that poker back where it was?' James Meade says.

'It's a pity you weren't as worried about the fire as the fucking poker!' Thomas says. 'Shush, now,' Delia says, picking up the poker and hanging it on its hook.

James Meade coughs deeply, rubs his marble eye, bangs his pipe on the table and looks out the window.

'Don't be banging your pipe at me!' Thomas says. Donie and Sam enter the back kitchen.

'Who do you think you are talking to him like that? Coming home acting the hard man, you big bollocks!' Donie says.

Through the back kitchen, Philly, Mary and Margaret pass, taking Barbara's hand as they go out the back door and into the back garden, down the path, through the white back gate and out into the back road.

Donie takes a grip of Thomas' head and Sam grabs Thomas' waist and they try to lift him off the ground. Thomas levers Donie around and flings him into the drinks cabinet, smashing a glass panel. James Meade stands up. Thomas swings Sam against the half-moon table beside Delia's armchair, Donie puts his arms around Thomas' neck, Sam swings his right fist connecting with Thomas' left eye socket, Thomas drives his right-hand knuckles upwards, they crack against Sam's chin. Sam and Donie somehow drag Thomas to the back door and out into the yard.

There is a good few minutes of punching and kicking and the three men walk slowly out the white back gate sometime later.

James Meade scratches his jaw, still standing at the round table in the front kitchen in the Bog Road.

The reel is over. Delia turns off the Grunow. She sweeps up the fragments of glass with the black steel brush and dustpan, part of the set which hangs on hooks on the red tiled mantelpiece, along with the poker.

13

It is not raining. Across the back garden wall, Joe Freeley whistles, pushing a wheelbarrow full of timbers toward his shed.

'What is he at now?' James Meade says. 'What is he doing with that type of a barrow, I wonder?'

Delia leaves her knitting needles hooked to a half-knitted cap on her lap. She looks across the front kitchen, past James Meade's silhouette to the sky beyond.

'He's a careful man,' Delia says.

'Arrah, he is an old stooge!' James Meade says.

Barbara comes home at half past three in the day, red ribbons swinging in her hair. She limps down the front hall, her back slanted forward.

'Brush your hair, Babba,' Delia says. 'Will you have a drop of soup?'

Barbara takes two onions from a basket on the counter in the back kitchen and skins them and chops them up on a wooden board and then she tosses them in the frying pan on the front left-hand hob of the cooker and stirs them around, turn and turn about, and then, when they are soft and beginning to brown, she puts them on a warmed plate and she brings them over to the round table and eats them all.

Afterwards, she runs out the back door and down the garden path and she looks out the white back gate, her ribbons on her shoulders and then she runs off down the back road in her awkward fashion, where there is the chatter of children somewhere below amongst the sunshine and the chimney smoke and the dogs barking.

Delia brings the plate and the cutlery and the frying pan and the wooden board to the sink in the back kitchen and washes them.

'He's going somewhere with the hedge clippers now. What hedge has he for cutting?' James Meade says.

Delia lies in the bed in the room in the house in the Country with her fingers intertwined together and the half-empty beaker of cold tea at an angle on the grey blanket. In front of her at the base of the bed, where the humming fridge should be, children play in the dim light of dusk in the Bog Road. They push and pull carts, tacked together from parts of fruit boxes, on modified bicycle axles with wheels off discarded toy trucks and cars. Most have dolls and teddies placed within, their paws hanging over the edge. Mary and Margaret and Kathleen pull one cart and Philly sits in the seat holding a doll. They shout and laugh and jump, ribbons torn from cheap cloth dance in their hair.

Barbara comes in the front hall with her schoolbag. Delia stirs cake mix around in a ceramic bowl at the counter in the back kitchen. James Meade sits at the round table by the tall window reading the newspaper. His pipe is in his mouth and a plume of smoke unfurls from it.

'That's it now mammy, I'm finished school forever! Woo-hoo!' Barbara jumps in the air awkwardly, her black tresses bounce in the sunlight from the tall window in the front kitchen in the house in the Bog Road.

'You want to go for a bit more schooling now,' James Meade says.

'What are you talking about Daddy, I'm getting a job, sure, I have no money!'

'What do you need money for?'

'Be as well to go and do nursing,' Delia says.

'Nursing? No thanks! A secretary job would be alright, though.'

'You're clever Barbara. You should go to college.'

'College? Who has time for that?' Barbara says. She sits on the armchair across from Delia. She slides off her sandals. Under the left big toe, a brown oval pad is strapped on. She pulls the pad off and massages the big toe and the top of the foot which is twisted to the left. Molly enters the back kitchen, holding a cigarette, wearing a mauve woollen dressing gown and a pair of red slippers.

'Are you not getting dressed at all today, Moll?' Barbara says.

'Actually, I was working all night,' Molly says.

A month later, Barbara leaves the house in the Bog Road at nine o'clock. She wears knee-high boots, a skirt three-quarters down her thighs, a yellow blouse tied with a two-inch grey belt across her waist. Her hair dangles past her elbows. Her blue eyes reflect the morning light. She hums as she walks down the Bog Road, a beige handbag rocking gently on her left arm.

At the mall, Barbara crosses to a block of offices beside the church, and enters through double doors. She sits at a desk on the second floor. She types.

'You should do a secretarial course,' someone whispers, looking at Barbara's half-typed letter. 'They are on at night, in Drum Street. That's too slow.'

A man of forty enters the office.

'Hello, girls, how are ye getting on?' he says, looking at Barbara. 'I was talking to Thomas last night in McCambridge's, gas man! Ye must come down for a drink this evening, ye'll get bored sitting at home, hah!' The man's laugh hangs as he walks out the doorway and down the carpeted hall.

Molly lives at home in the house in the Bog Road. She works in the bacon factory, usually on the night shift. She has green eyes and thick black curls around her shoulders. She seems to see things in corners. She taps the banister with care as she comes down the stairs in the afternoons, sometimes stops in the front hall, turns, walks halfway up the stairs, taps the banister with care and comes down. Delia can see this from the sink in the back kitchen as she takes the frying pan from the first press beside the cooker underneath the counter.

Molly takes clothes from a yellow trunk in the back room and brings them downstairs to the bathroom and washes them in the bath with flaked washing agent.

'Did they need washing?' Delia says.

Molly sits at the round table in the front kitchen and smokes cigarettes, placing each butt at a different side of the square glass ashtray.

'Where is Barbara?' Molly says.

'She is working today,' Delia says, tidying the counter, straightening the vegetable basket, the white delph teapot, the bread bin pushed against the yellow patterned tiles.

'She is gone with my yellow blouse again,' Molly says, looking out the tall window at the tops and skirts on the washing line lifting gently in the wind. 'The rotten bitch.'

Thomas comes home at different times. He does not always come at Christmas and Easter, not anymore. He could arrive in February, stay for six weeks and leave the week before Easter. One year, he came in the middle of December and left the day before Christmas Eve.

'What is wrong with that man?' James Meade says.

When Thomas is home, he gets up at ten o'clock and walks to Ryan's Road. He goes to the pub across from the cinema and drinks successive pints of Guinness. Thin and fat pale-faced men walk in and out of the pub all day to and from the bookies next door with yellow slips of paper and glowing cigarettes.

Thomas comes home at night, singing, shouting in the front bed-room, James Meade pretending he is asleep, Delia looking at their son, Thomas squeezing her hand, tears falling down his face, beer on his shirt, his teeth a light brown, mumbling 'aah…that fuck-ing…ahhh…ahh…that bit…ahhh…ya…' leaning closer to Delia, out of the light of the landing, becoming a dark shape, blocking out the doorway behind him, his thick fingers on her shoulder, warm tears on her hands, dripping from the dark space nodding in front of her.

'Aaah…aaahh…aaahhhaaahhhaaahhh…aaahh…Tony…fucking council, twas their fault…did not think a young lad would…ahh …ahhahhaaa…Bartholomew…Barry…she is a bitch…a bitch…'

Delia is not sure of what her son is saying. She can never be sure with Thomas, because some nights he is different, not crying, he is shouting, runs up the stairs, bursts in the door of the front bedroom, hauls James Meade out of the bed and pushes him up against the wardrobe, coathangers rattle within.

'You let my brother die!' Thomas says. Delia stands beside him, pulling at his arm, Donie comes in and there is a flash of fists and blood and the wardrobe is on the bed and James Meade and Delia get out of the front bedroom and they have to sleep downstairs that night.

Sometimes Thomas stays in the house in the Bog Road all day. These days, he cannot sit in one room for longer than a few minutes. He is on the armchair in the front kitchen, now he leans on the coun-ter in the back kitchen. He stands at the pedestal in the bathroom, smoking a cigarette, now he sits at the round table, leafing through a book, then sitting at the piano in the front room, tapping the keys aimlessly.

He looks out the front door, now looking up, then down the Bog Road. 'Wasters!' he says, as he turns in and walks down the front hall to the back kitchen and looks at the red tiled mantelpiece, where De-lia sits darning a sock.

'Who are?' Delia says.

'The crowd out there,' Thomas says. 'Ma, have you got a few bob on you?'

'For what?'

'I have to go down the town and meet a fella about work and I wouldn't like to be stuck.'

When Barbara comes home from work, Thomas sits at the round table. 'Watch out for them fellas,' he says. 'Be careful. After one thing. Degenerates a lot of them.'

'I'm fine, thanks,' Barbara says.

'You think you're fine. But don't walk alone at night. Dangerous around here. Bastards a lot of them.' Thomas stares out the tall window. Joe Freeley walks slowly along the garden path next door, pushing his green wheelbarrow. His whistling can be heard in the front kitchen of the house in the Bog Road.

'What is that Freeley at now?' he says.

'Couldn't tell ya,' James Meade says, filling his pipe at the other side of the round table.

Thomas talks to James Meade in the back garden. Arms and voices are raised. Delia cannot hear what is being said. Thomas points to the top of the hedge. James Meade shakes his head, rubs his chest and walks toward the shed.

'He won't let me cut the fecking hedge. I "do it uneven", d'ya ever hear the likes!' Thomas sits at the round table. He taps his fingers.

'Do you have a few bob, ma, I have to go down the town?'

'Did you get my letters when you were beyont?'

'Huh? What letters?'

'The letters I sent you. Are you still in Nasmyth Street?'

'Yeah.'

'42 A?'

'Yeah.'

'And you never got my letters?'

'Oh, I did, ma. I did. Thanks.'

'And you wouldn't think of sending me one back?'

'Ah, ma, come on, sure I do have no time for writing letters over there. I do be flat out.'

They sit alone. The sunlight streams through the tall window facing out into the yard. Light is split by the wooden bars around the panes. A fly walks along the shoulder of James Meade as he stares at the brown patterned carpet from the chair at the round table in the front kitchen in the house in the Bog Road.

A telegram lies in front of him. Part of it is folded toward the red tiled mantelpiece where Delia sits. She can read some of the lines '– identified as Donald Abraham Meade, 6 Hatton Drive, Hammersmith, Borough of London, and formerly of 109, Bog Road–'.

It is over now, Delia sits alone, James Meade is not there. It is over now, she does not sit in her armchair at the red tiled mantelpiece, she lies in the bed in the room in the house in the Country.

Delia can hear noises at two o'clock in the darkness.

'Really…yeah…mm…okay…'

'Geraghty…really…yeah…really…'

'Stop it!' Barbara says. There is a clack. There are footsteps. The front door to the house in the Bog Road bangs shut.

Delia hears Barbara cry. She looks across at James Meade. His breath is broken, not smooth. He coughs often throughout the night. She has asked him to go to the Doctor. 'Bleddy doctors,' James Meade says.

Delia gets up slowly and pads down the stairs to the front kitchen. Barbara stares out the tall window to the yard and sky beyond. 'It's alright, lovin', everything will work out, you'll see,' Delia says.

'They are just so mean, mammy!' Barbara says, leaning her head toward Delia's abdomen. Delia stands beside the chair at the round table, rubbing Barbara's back in the blue light.

The Bog Road sleeps. Streetlights throw a yellow glow on each terrace. Motor cars pass more often now. James Meade tosses and turns in the front bedroom. Delia wakens. 'An awful pain in me side,' James Meade says.

'Do you want to go down and get an aspirin?' Delia says.

James Meade goes downstairs. Delia hears him at the last press over the counter in the back kitchen, dropping a tablet in a glass, pouring in water, stirring it. He swallows, gulping.

James Meade still has the pain the next day. He sits at the round table, rubbing his side every few minutes, his pipe lying unlit, his newspaper folded, unread.

'Jesus!' he says, at one part of the morning.

'You might go to the doctor, Jimmy,' Delia says.

'I might. Bleddy doctors!' James Meade says.

The next day, Barbara comes home from work at half past four. Delia stands at the front door. 'He died in his sleep,' Delia says.

'Changing the furniture is a good thing to do after a loss in the house,' Mrs Freeley says, sucking on a More. Frankie comes with his white Escort van to take the half-moon table to the dump.

117

'How are you keeping, Delia?' Frankie says, as he wrestles with the awkwardly shaped object.

'Keeping going, Francis.'

'Aye. A fair old shock to ye all.'

'Can you move that television over there?'

'No bother, Delia.'

Frankie sits in the Escort, swigs from a hip flask and starts the engine. He drives down the Bog Road, the half-moon table juts out the back, the two back doors tied across it.

Delia buys a two-seater couch at a jumble sale down the town. Barbara comes home in the evening. She is cross.

'Where is the table, mammy?'

'I got rid of it.'

'But Daddy loved that table. How could you do that? And why is the television like that?'

'Leave her alone,' Molly says, a cigarette in her mouth, her hair tangled, her mauve dressing gown tied loosely around her.

'Mind your own business, lying in bed all day, while I'm out working.'

'I worked long enough! Leave mammy alone,' Molly says. 'And leave Jimmy Murphy alone too.'

'What? Do you own him or something?'

'Anyway, didn't go too well last night by the sounds of it.'

'Mind your own business!' Barbara goes upstairs, her feet banging the stair threads.

'Will you leave her?' Delia says.

A man comes into the front kitchen of the house in the Bog Road. He is of medium height, has bushy black hair with a neat goatee and green eyes. Barbara holds his hand. 'This is Aidan, mammy.' Barbara says.

'Hello, Aidan,' Delia says. Aidan shakes her hand.

'Nice to meet you, Delia,' Aidan says.

'Aidan is from the Country,' Barbara says, placing her beige handbag on the two-seater and sitting on the armchair opposite Delia. Aidan sits on the two-seater beside the handbag.

'Nice house you have, Delia,' Aidan says, looking around.

James Meade was toasted at the wedding. Sam did not come. There was no reply to the letters sent to his address in Australia. Kathleen did not come from Watford.

'You can't bate the red mate,' Thomas says during the meal, drinking from a glass of whiskey.

Aidan moves into the Bog Road. He leaves every day for the Country. He gets up at half past eight and puts on his corduroy trousers, his loose shirt, his round topped hat. He kisses Barbara goodbye in the back room. He drives down the Bog Road in his father's Morris Minor, to walk the fields in the Country.

Molly stirs in the box room. She moved in there after the wedding. She could no longer share the back room as Aidan had moved in.

Barbara sits in the front kitchen on the two-seater after work. Molly sits at the round table. Delia sits on her armchair at the red tiled mantelpiece. They are watching the news on the Bush television set.

'That news is depressing,' Barbara says. She gets up and turns off the television.

'I was watching that!' Molly says.

'Shush!' says Delia.

Molly turns the television on. The news is over.

'Over now. What a bitch!' Molly says. Aidan comes into the front kitchen. He kisses Barbara and sits next to her on the two-seater.

'How did you get on today, Aidan?' Delia says.

'Good. Nice day today,' Aidan says. Molly goes out the back door, walks down the path, to the white back gate, looks down the back road, then up.

'I was at the doctor today,' Barbara says.

Molly turns around, looks through the tall window, over the round table to where Delia and Barbara are hugging each other and then Aidan hugs Delia and they are all smiling. Molly looks to the sky, there are a few clouds, it is getting dark. She tosses her cigarette to the ground and walks down the back road.

14.

Delia sits on her armchair at the red tiled mantelpiece in the front kitchen of the house in the Bog Road. In her arms, wrapped in a blue soft cloth is Barbara's first child. The baby's green eyes dart around the front kitchen. Delia holds him close to her bosom, rocking him gently.

Now she leaves the baby into the carrycot on the brown patterned carpet in front of her armchair. She stands at the counter in the back kitchen, putting a spoon of sugar and a small amount of warm water from the brown kettle into one of the bottles of milk Barbara leaves on the counter every morning.

In Delia's arms, the baby wraps his lips around the teat, sucking from the bottle, his eyes widening a little as the milk enters his stomach.

In the evening Barbara comes home, dropping her beige handbag on the two-seater, sitting beside it and taking out a cigarette. The baby is asleep in Delia's arms.

'Gerard pinched me behind again today,' Barbara says.

'Is there no one you could go to about him?' Delia says.

'Sure he's the boss, mammy,' Barbara says.

'Maybe Aidan could have a word with him?' Delia says.

'Aidan wouldn't say boo to a goose,' Barbara says.

Aidan comes home in the evening. His shirt sleeves are rolled to his elbows, strands of hay stick to his loose trousers. He takes up the baby from the carrycot and hugs him tightly.

'How are you today, Mr Baby?' Aidan says.

The child is two years old. He has dark hair. Delia holds a beaker of orange to his lips. She unscrews the lid of the beaker and, taking a Liga biscuit from a plate on the black hearth, she dips it in the orange for a moment and then offers it to the child's mouth. He parts his lips, showing stumps of teeth and sucks at the softened biscuit, crumbs fall onto his bib. He chews and swallows.

Afterwards, Delia lifts the child up, noticing his weight now, his arms and legs waving helplessly in midair, she pulls him to her chest, her green cardigan rubbing against his cheek, and she moves slowly from left to right and right to left, humming a tune she invents in her mind, an amalgamation of melodies she has heard on the Grunow over many years. The child is asleep. She kisses him on the cheek, his skin is smooth and soft.

Molly has taken redundancy from the bacon factory. Now she gets up at eleven and drinks tea and smokes cigarettes at the round table in the chair where James Meade used to sit and read the newspaper and look out the tall window at Joe Freeley pushing a wheelbarrow full of timbers toward his shed.

Every day Molly takes up the child and rocks him and feeds him his orange and Liga biscuits or his mashed-up potatoes, or mashed-up carrots or, when he has some teeth, chopped-up sausage. She feeds it to him slowly, rubbing his head. Now Molly sits at the round table, rocking the child in her arms. Delia knits in her armchair beside the red tiled mantelpiece.

'This will be a lovely cap for winter,' Delia says. 'The light blue looks nice on him.'

'You're not knitting him another one, mammy?'

'Those ones don't really fit him anymore, he's growing so fast.'

'Mmm, the weight of him now sure,' Molly says. She puts the child back into the blue wooden playpen and as she does she makes a low grunt.

'What is it?' Delia says.

'An awful dart in me side,' Molly says.

'Indigestion,' Delia says.

Some weeks later, Molly rubs her side again as she rocks the child in her arms at the round table. 'You don't still have that pain, do you?' Delia says.

'Worse now it is.'

'You better go into Trien. Probably all that stooping for years in the bacon factory.'

Molly presses her top front teeth against her lower lip and looks out the window. Molly comes home from the doctor with a packet of tablets.

'Says he doesn't know what it is. Probably a pulled muscle. He gave me painkillers.'

The child is at the armchair across from Delia. He lifts his right hand off the armrest and stands independently, before toppling over onto the brown patterned carpet. 'Look it, mammy, he was standing there!' Molly says.

Molly's pain gets worse. At night, Delia is woken by Molly's groans. Molly sleeps with Delia in the front bedroom since the child moved into the box room. Aidan has painted the box room yellow and has written the child's name over the door in thick blue strokes.

Molly has tests in the hospital. A week later, she goes to see Dr Trien again. She comes back and sits at the round table, her fingers intertwined on her lap. Her large green eyes seem moist and look directly at Delia. Through the tall window, Delia can see the ends of the sheets lifting on the washing line in the light morning breeze. 'I asked him how much good the treatment would be and he said it was hard to say...I said would I...I...be hard to see...living for a long time...and he said he didn't know. So it looks...bad, mammy.' There is a noise upstairs. Barbara is closing the tall shiny teak wardrobe in the back room. The child is in the back kitchen trying to walk. He lifts his right foot and moves it forward, holding onto the last drawer handle beside the sink. He lunges, letting go of the handle, stepping forward before falling gently on the orange linoleum in the back kitchen.

Delia sits back in her armchair. Molly lights a cigarette. She sucks the smoke deep into her lungs and exhales it into the swirling dust in the front kitchen in the house in the Bog Road.

It is morning. The daylight is dull from the tall window. A dog barks in the back road. Delia sits in her armchair at the red tiled mantelpiece. Her left hand is within a grey sock, the right hand directs a needle around a small hole near the toe. The child sits in his small chair in front of Delia's armchair. He plays with a wooden train. Heels move around the brown patterned carpet. Molly stands at the round table, taking the lid off the stainless steel teapot.

'Will you let it draw,' Delia says. 'It will be like water.'

'I just want to stir it, to hurry it up, I have to go,' Molly says, holding a tablespoon in her right hand.

'Where are you going all dolled up this morning?' Delia says.

The child drops the train and cries out. Molly lies on the brown patterned carpet beside the round table. Delia gets up, walks out through the front kitchen, the back kitchen, the front hall, the front garden, onto the street and in the white front gate to 108 and knocks on the front door. Charles Freeley is home. He calls for an ambulance on their telephone. Molly is dead.

Dark walls and ceilings.

Gold cigarette box.

Table.

Cereal.

Near the coast, the wind blows through all of the branches of the trees. The leaves lift from the nothing visible. The thicker branches move in heavier gusts. The sun is warm. There are no clouds. Only a base from which to draw.

Delia's dress is bright blue with white flowers. Her arms are hairless and browned from the great summers that the country has in these days. Maisie wears a bright blue dress but on hers there are butterflies. The grass tickles their knees as they walk along.

'That is a ring in there,' Maisie says. 'You can't stand in it, Dee, or The Shee will take you away.'

'Is that true, though?' Delia says.

'It is. One day, I was walking here alone and a man came along and he was wearing a long black cape and a hood and he was reading a book and he asked me to come with him.'

'But when was this, we always walk together?'

'One day, we didn't. One day, I was walking here alone and a man came along. He was wearing a long black cape and a hood and he was holding a big hook thing and he asked me to come with him!'

It rains, in black elastic droplets, sticking to them, to their dresses, their faces, to the trees, the stone walls, the clay track darkens to red, to black, and they are lost, running through charred grass, through soot, through dust.

The dream is over. Delia has moved on to another place. It is a carnival, people laugh and clap each other's backs, and hand money and take goods and Delia walks along in summer sandals, her footprints outlined in the dust. She straightens her long brown hair, adjusting a hairgrip on her crown. The heat of the sun rolls on her cheeks. Men at each stall look up as she walks past. At the corner of the field is the horseshoe stall.

Delia stands there, watching the children come and hand pennies to the man behind the worn wooden table. He gives them a horseshoe from a pile beside his money box. They toss it, trying to hook it around the tall wooden pole behind the man. At the side of the stall are soft, fluffy teddy bears, wooden trains, raggedy dolls.

James Meade comes walking, smiling, his cap crooked on his head, a trace of stubble on his jaw, his eyes are blue.

'I was watching you,' James Meade says. He takes her hand but she pulls away.

'Jimmy, we are out in public!'

123

'Arrah, what do these crowd care! Come on!' James Meade says and they walk past the attractions, talking of this and that, the crowd, the day, the week. Delia is saying something when the leaves all fall at once from the trees, the field and everything in it is swept away like an incoming wave covers sand along a beach.

'Take one of these every day. They will minimise the discomfort,' Dr Crabbe is saying. Delia nods and holds her black handbag tight on her lap.

Delia takes the pink pill every morning before breakfast with a glass of water. Now she feels it travelling down her throat, through her intestines, breaking up, the white powder intermingling with her blood stream, the chemicals within finding their way to the umbilical cord and down the shoot, into the unborn, into the body, finding their way, twisting, turning, grooving.

There was no baby there, there was a baby there. There was no way of knowing, there was a way of knowing. But Dr Crabbe did not know. The embryo is awoken from its sleep, it swims in the uterus, the spine twisting, limbs rupturing.

Delia stares at the ceiling in the room in the Country. The foetus curled up, sleeping like the kitten, defenceless, attacked, torn to pieces and mashed together again with some parts missing, a secondary attempt, no, not that bad. Only contortions, physical and mental. Delia sighs and looks around the room. The room is empty. She needs to urinate, she needs to eat, she needs to waken, she needs to sleep. She needs to move and stop. It was not her fault. It was nobody's fault. It was Dr Crabbe. The man was an imbecile. But he did not know. He did not know he was an imbecile. Delia shivers, tries to move further down the bed, the blankets over her, the top of the sheet wrapped tightly around her fingers. Dr Crabbe floats above her, with an axe over the kitten under the pink blanket. Delia wants to stop Dr Crabbe, he is not moving, nothing moves, nothing changes, nothing stays the same.

The boy will come soon, she knows, she hopes. It is time for her tea. She may have had her tea a few minutes ago. She looks to see if there are any crumbs stuck to the blanket. There are. But they could be there a long time. She looks back at the poster on the ceiling. The kitten is still there. Dr Crabbe is not there anymore.

It is winter. The weather has gotten worse. The rain bangs against Delia's window. The boy comes into the room in the house in the

Country. He carries a small box wrapped in paper with hollies on it. He hands the box to Delia, and kisses her on the lips, the hairs on the space between her upper lip and her nose prickling against his smooth skin. Delia takes the letter from Philly. Her cousin, Megan, has written from Boston. It is always sunny in Boston but it snows in the winter. There is always work in Boston. There are big motor cars in Boston, big buildings, everything is better, everything is faster, everything is different, everything is better. Delia opens the package slowly. An electricity bill. 'Bleddy electric,' James Meade says, coughing and lighting his pipe and looking in the newspaper at the round table in the front room in the house on the Bog Road. In the box there is a red and white grooming set, a comb, hairbrush and mirror, the colours blend across the items as though they were marble. Delia smiles. 'A nice idea,' she says.

The ground underneath them begins to vibrate and the walls get soft and bend and the ceiling runs off into the sky leaving the air outside to come in gusts to the room. Delia and the boy melt into the beige linoleum, merging into the concrete, becoming part of the solidity, all of the room disappears down a sinkhole forming in the ground.

The snap of the door latch resounds through the house when the boy leaves Delia's room. He turns on the Bush television in the recessed section of his bedroom, an area designed for a wardrobe to be fitted, but never was. MTV is on and music plays and girls dance around, girls older than him and he stares at the screen.

In the bed across the room, the boy's brother sleeps and his sister plays with a doll and a teddy in the next bedroom and Aidan is gone somewhere and Barbara is at college studying for something and Delia coughs and splutters in her room. The boy gets off the bed and pulls up the brown patterned carpet at a corner and urinates. The urine steams and the flow seems to run for a long time. When he is finished, he rolls back the brown patterned carpet on the soaked concrete and sits on his bed and watches the Bush television.

The programme is about two men entering a long tunnel and from here they can travel to other places in other times, but the programme itself is not of his time, it is in the past too, twenty years or more. He does not much like programmes of his own time, he looks for these programmes in the TV guide. He wants to go in the tunnel, he considers building a tunnel like the one on the television.

In another programme, men were fighting invading aliens and the only route to attack the alien spaceship was through a long tunnel, which had a ray of light running along the sides that vaporised any humans that entered. But the humans were somehow able to turn off the ray for a certain period of time and use the tunnel to get to the enemy ship. If they did not get through before the time was up, the rays would come back on and vaporise them. The boy is scared of this tunnel. At night he imagines being stuck in the tunnel and trying to get out, to get out in time before the lethal rays return.

As he lies in the bed, he pushes his right arm across his body underneath him and swings his torso over and back, back and over. Images pass through his head.

There is a need to make sound, and he begins to hum as he has done for years, he has done this since he was in the bed in the box room in the house on the Bog Road. He rocks and hums and hums and the humming becomes words, songs of a sort.

'Aaah…aaaahhhaaa…aahhaaa…aahhaahhaahh…hahahah…haha …aaaahhhhaaaa…aahhaaa…aahhaahhaahh…hahahah…hahahahahah ahah…aaahhhhaaaa huhhhahhuhhuhhh.'

His body releases the tightness it had not felt until now, he smiles, his eyes closed, seeing images, grass, people holding hands, cars, trains, television programmes, schoolteachers, football posters on the walls of his room, passing through his mind.

The boy runs around the odd shaped garden in front of the house in the Country. He kicks the ball to the sky, it bounces off the electric cables. He looks through the top of the hedge, of the trees in the garden. The trees were not climbable. Other boys he knew climbed other trees. But the trees in the garden could not be climbed.

'Shanz to Rollerio, the new Brazilian signing. This move has potential for United,' Pete Popse says.

Through the open window, Delia hears the noise of the ball, kicked hard against the two-foot bank at the hedge in the odd shaped garden, with the gentle slope across the middle and the large rock in the corner. She hears the boy talk. She imagines his cheeks red, his fringe moist against his forehead.

The boy shoots at the two-foot bank. Bang-bang, bang-bang-bang. Bang-bang, bang-bang-bang.

126

15.

It is April. The boy gets off the school bus. He is hungry and tired. There are images flying through his head, skirts, blonde hair, chatter, chatter, chatter. There is an ambulance outside the front door of the house in the Country.

A dark dye rises up through his body like liquid soot, poring through the flesh, taking over his whole being. He feels shaky, like he is being shamed. He throws his schoolbag across his shoulder and walks in the twisting drive through the odd shaped garden.

Somewhere, blasts of colour and black and grey and other unfathomable shapes and sounds flash. Maisie turns into a goat-like creature, laughing, trying to choke Delia beside an ass and cart on fair day. Delia's body grew out of itself in the struggle and welds to wooden water barrels and trailers of turf.

The world was becoming rubber and making twanging noises as if it was being stretched too much, like an elastic band that would soon snap, the waiting for it to snap, the waiting for her to snap.

Delia's mother and father are on the street, their faces grow long into the sky, their eyes pop out of their skulls and roll around on the ground, clinking together like marbles. Trees in the fields grow up to the sky becoming howling dragon-like creatures.

The Bog Road sinks to the ground, hissing like the air coming from a tyre, the houses one strangely shaped bicycle tube deflating. Mr Flounders, the rope still around his neck, his face a rubber blue, bangs the ground with his turf scraped fist, cursing. Bones push up through the soft crust, circling around Mr Flounders, they arrange into skeletons, flesh, blood, skin grows on the bones, figures now in rags, moaning, chanting, humming.

Delia sees many groups in the Bog Road, an area of marshy ground and murky pools, wooden cabins overlook the scene, children lie on the peat with rushes in their mouths and Mr Flounders bangs the ground again.

The football pitch beyond lifts up toward the sky and slides down like a condemned ship to the waters underneath.

Everything sinks. Gravity seems to survive the parameters of the dream world.

Delia has had a bad night. She has a sour taste in her throat when she wakes and launches into the daily ritual of coughing, the unbreakably anchored phlegm in her larynx resisting hours of attack from lung-propelled air pockets.

It is all a montage of memories now, she cannot untangle it. There is nothing more for her to do here, in this place. Delia thinks she would be better off somewhere else, somewhere where there was no need of breathing, of coughing, of thinking.

There is a lot of movement today in the house in the Country. Nothing moves, yet there is movement somewhere. Sounds. A phone call. A low conversation. Zips and bag handles. Suitcase wheels. Zips again. Delia looks toward the door. It opens, men in plastic green jackets enter. The war has arrived in Ireland. Hitler has invaded. Delia looks around for James Meade. One of the men puts a plastic triangle over Delia's mouth. 'Can you hear me, Delia?' he says, lifting the triangle for a moment and then returning it to her mouth. Warm air fills her lungs. Barbara and Aidan stand at the door, like two scared cats, Delia thinks, she tries to laugh, wants to laugh out loud.

'She is okay, Barbara.'

'Thank you, thanks a million.'

Delia is falling, a vehicle moves, everything blurs, colours, it is all just one or two colours, now it is all white, the whiteness becomes brighter, liquid whiteness from the triangle pours into her mouth, warming her whole body. She tries to speak but cannot. She feels as though flung through the universe in some pod around and around, she has nowhere to go, she has no one to help her, to stop her, twisting and turning through galaxies of stars. She is wearing a green gown, she is lying on a bed, she is getting up, she is getting married today. There are many flowers. Girls laugh in a group somewhere, children, their hair tied up in ribbons, relations of James Meade's.

James Meade will be at the church in his best suit, one of his brothers has the ring, it will be a great day. There is a smell of whiskey, one of the bridesmaids, her sister Kathleen, carries a glass into their mother and father's bedroom in the thatched cottage near the sea. 'I hope the ring will fit you, Dee,' Kathleen says, doing something with Delia's hair, straightening it out down her back. 'Go on, drink that down you, it'll settle the nerves...' Kathleen hands Delia the glass. Delia looks at her hand, there is something wrong, the wedding ring is already on her finger, her hands are wrinkled, shrivelled up, there are pocks below her knuckles...how can she go to the church like that?

Delia looks around the white pod, a man in a green jacket reads a newspaper. The house in the Country does not have Delia in it, not anymore. The boy walks down the long hall past Delia's room. She is not dead. She might come back. She might not.

In the County Home the mind closes down, shuts up. There is no more forward or back, no present or past. The boy thinks about this as he runs out of the empty house into the odd shaped garden with his ball. 'Jack Raker to Bannister now, nice pass, Rovers are coming into the game...cross oh, great stop by the keeper, gives it straight to his captain, who takes it and runs, goes past one, and another...different class...such elegance...what a goal, making it 2-0, just what United needed! The man is simply an artist. There is no other word for him...' Pete Popse says.

The boy visits the County Home. The ceilings are high. Blue uniformed staff keep their mouths tightly closed. Delia lies in a ward with eleven others. She sleeps, her fingers intertwined over a grey blanket. The sheets are white. The curtain which can be drawn around the bed at certain times, other times, is cream. The walls are grey. The window frames are grey aluminium. The floor is grey linoleum. The head of Delia's bed is a white metal frame. Beside the bed, there is a grey steel locker. On top there is a newspaper and an empty plastic beaker and at the back, an unopened bottle of Lucozade. On the wall across is a white-faced clock with plain black numerals. The bed continually tilts, humming as it does. It turns until it reaches thirty degrees, then it turns back the other way.

'For bed sores,' someone says. The boy and his sister stand at the end of the bed, watching the bed moving, whirring. The younger boy leans against the chair where Barbara sits. Aidan stands beside her. He is scratching his beard.

'Looks great!' Barbara says.

'A lot improved,' Aidan says.

'She'll live to a hundred!' Barbara says.

Delia has a thick tube running to her right nostril, her face is pale, saliva spills slowly from her lips. The boy is alone, there are people with him, he is alone. He watches the bed moving, slowly up and around and down, and turning back again, and up and around and down and turning back, whirring, humming. Delia does not look worried. The boy does not have to feed her digestive biscuits anymore. He can do nothing for her, not now, not anymore.

The twelve of them lie in their beds, heedless of the people who come and go. There is a cough, the prolonged clearing of a throat. The wheedling of a Zimmer frame passing in the hall. Delia does not need a Zimmer frame, not anymore.

Cars drive past on the road beyond the car park of the County Home. People meet and shake hands at the entrance doors and talk and laugh. The boy looks out past the car park, under the cloudy sky, to the town. Delia does not live within the Town, not now, not anymore.

In Delia's mind there is dark quietness. There are the membranes and the blood vessels and the tissue. Sounds fade and lights dim like the Bush television set in the front kitchen in the house in the Bog Road. Colours vanishing from the top and bottom, meeting in the middle, a thin line in the blackness, decreasing from either side to a white dot before, in a flash, fading out.

Colours are not present now, in her mind, only darks, not blacks or greys only darks. Air travels in and out of the larynx with difficulty. Delia's chest rises and falls, her bed turns from left to right.

One of the blue uniformed staff walks around the ward, writing on a hanging board at the end of each bed, now moving a trolley, now pouring a beaker of orange into the mouth of a woman in the bed next to Delia. It reminds the boy of dosing calves with Aidan in the Country.

On the way back, they pass the house in the Bog Road. At the junction, the boy looks through the glass down the street. It is silent in the front kitchen in the house in the Bog Road.

The boy sits at the square table in the kitchen in the house in the Country, looking at a textbook and then writing in an exercise book with a blue biro. The biro also has the option of writing in red. He uses the red ink for drawing in the margin that he must adhere to as he starts each sentence. He also draws a red line across the top of the page. As he answers each question in the textbook, there is a weakness, in his legs, in his chest, there is something not together, like he is pulling tug-o-war and the rope is loose, or the rope is broken. Something, somewhere is not connected. He feels weaker as he writes on the page, a third of the way down, something slows, something within, his writing fades, he begins to drift, drift away.

In the odd shaped garden the boy can run around and commentate on 'Raker' passing to 'Bannister' and 'a wonderful piece of skill' creating 'a perfect goal.'

He lies in bed, staring at the ceiling, thinking of Delia in her bed in the County Home, swivelling from left to right, waiting to go to the Otherplace, and wondering when his time will come to go to the Otherplace and what the Otherplace might be.

He rocks over and back and over and back and chants and hums and thinks about people and places, television programmes and footballers and schoolgirls and anything which Delia cannot think about, not now, not anymore. He can get away from the thoughts of the Otherplace for now, remove Delia from his mind, for the moment. He can walk past the room Delia slept in for years without looking in, he does not go in there, not now, not anymore.

In the morning, the house is silent. Barbara and Aidan are locked in a spoon position. Aidan whispers in Barbara's ear.

The boy dreams of the opposite sex in some form of mangled pile. There is a fierce clutch of arms and legs, a sweating, heaving mass of flesh and bone. Squashed together, chasing something, chasing anything. Underneath the bodies is nothing, nothing supports them, then only wires and broken glass.

The image switches to the push of foreign skin on his skin, the clash and connection of eyes reflecting a golden light, the fusion of independent minds through an unidentifiable conduit.

The younger boy lies with his mouth open. His soft skin still, his eyes closed. He does not move all night except to breathe, unlike his brother, who twists constantly to find a position of comfort. Above the younger boy's bed, there is a shelf the older brother fitted some years earlier, using a picture book for instruction. He had hammered three-inch steel nails through the two-by-one white deal, knocking lumps of plaster from the wall.

'What are you doing?' Aidan had said. The boy had cut a curved bracket with a coping saw and fitted it to the end of the shelf.

On the bracket, there is a red round sticker. The boy's uncle Joseph had been running for election and he had given Barbara's children a box of campaign stickers to circulate in the village in the Country. The sticker has an image of the party leader and underneath a slogan: 'A voice that will be heard!'

In the next bedroom, the girl is asleep. Her nose is blocked and the air gets caught in the channels to the lungs. On the locker beside her, there is a bottle of Epilym. In one corner of the ceiling, there is a long novelty stamp the boy stuck some years earlier of a train leaving a station. The boy and the girl had shared this room until the third child was born. In the room at the top of the long hall, there is no one sleeping. The tall shiny teak wardrobe's door is open, Delia's gabardine jacket hangs on the rail. The bed has been stripped of blankets, only the rubber cover on the mattress remains. The Zimmer frame lies on the floor beside the humming fridge.

The boy awakens, his eyes adjust to the morning light. His mind recalls the dream he was having, recreating the soft outline of images and sounds in his head. He takes a magazine from a cardboard box under the bed.

It is a television guide. He looks for the fashion section. Here, there are photos of models wearing medium length skirts and shoulder-less tops.

While he proceeds, he keeps an eye on the door, his most terrified imagination pictures a bewildered expression on Aidan's face looking straight at him in mid-thrust. His sheets are stained. He wonders what Barbara makes of them. He imagines she thinks some urine petered from him in the midst of the night.

He sees the skin of the fashion models, their clothes being peeled away and he absorbing what lies beneath. He feels strangely satisfied, but a curious sense of guilt floods him. He feels he has something to hide, something that cannot be spoken of.

He watches television in the dining room. There is a phone call. They drive into the town in Aidan's light blue Kadett hatchback. They park outside the County Home.

It is morning. Delia believes it is morning. She opens her eyes. The light is dark.

Those in the other beds are asleep. They may be dead. Delia opens and closes her mouth. She cannot move her fingers but that is not important now.

Delia is at a carnival. There are many rides to go on. Wedding guests in formal clothes are on the swing boats, there goes Uncle Tommy! On the roundabout Maisie and Peggy McHale whizz around and around, waving to Delia who walks toward them holding a stick of candy floss. Candy floss!

A man throws a horseshoe. It catches the top of the wooden pole and slides down. There is a round of applause. But there are no prizes at the side of the stall. No dolls, no teddy bears. Where are the dolls? Where are the teddy bears? Delia shouts. The man behind the worn wooden table looks at her blankly. He takes a child from somewhere, boy or girl, Delia cannot say which, and he hands it to the winner. The winner walks away, holding the child's arm, looking back at Delia.

Peggy McHale and Maisie have ran off from the roundabout and Delia walks in her summer dress with strawberries in a cluster, this pattern repeated again and again.

Delia finds the dodgems, go-carts with little wheels pedalled around a fenced area, boys shout as they collide with each other.

'Watch out, watch out!' Delia's mother and father say from the fence.

Further on is a tent. 'The Crystal Ball' is written on a sign hanging over the door. Through a chink of light between purple curtains, Delia sees a woman in her thirties sitting at a round table, a bald man, much older, sits across, dressed in black, speaking quietly.

In the corner of the field, 'Shop of Horrors' is painted across a board over a curtained doorway to a black wooden shed. Delia hands a coin to a man and walks through the black curtain. The ground disappears underneath her, green figures laugh into her face, Delia is falling but remains upright, voices scream soundlessly around her.

Maisie lies in a white coffin on the ground below. Delia tries to get up, tries to get to the black curtain.

In the field, Delia drifts around, as though floating, not touching the ground and Maisie and Peggy McHale join her and the three of them run, trying out all the swings and rides and the candy floss, a piece sticks to Maisie's nose, Delia laughs, she laughs and laughs until her jaw gets sore.

Delia buys an ice cream from her schoolteacher, it tastes of gravel. The clouds move quickly, like they are sheep rushing through a gap in a stone wall to a sweet meadow. Delia wants to speak, a man brings a soapbox, a crowd of people gather in front of her, there is a round of applause, she is asked to begin. She opens her mouth, but nothing comes out, yet the people are nodding, everything is right, everything is as it should be.

The fairground melts into rectangles of colours, like a cityscape and Delia is a giant, she can see over everything, and it softens into a blurry whirl. Delia is floating like Dorothy in the hurricane, spinning around and around, except she is not in a house, she is out in the open, everything swirls around her like it is all lost, this is the place lost things go, everything is lost here, found, lost, open, closed.

Delia is hungry. 'Is there breakfast?' she says, when the blue uniformed figure comes near. A bowl of porridge on a tray. A plastic spoon pushed to her lips. The food is in her mouth. It will not go down her throat. Something gets stuck in the air channel, she coughs.

Delia sees a flash of silver, somewhere, in the middle of her vision. 'You're married?'

'I am indeed, Delia. Two years now, for my sins.'

The spoon is at Delia's lips. 'Do you want to try swallowing that porridge?'

The blue figure moves away.

'I wouldna say that.'

'What's that, Delia?'

Delia feels the porridge slide down her throat. She licks her lip. 'It is no sin to…to do.'

'Well done, Delia.'

After the bowl is taken away, Delia can see better. Things clear up. It was all a silly dream, all silly nightmares. Everything is alright now. Barbara would be here soon. She was just forgetful, that was all. Soon, she would go home to the house in the Bog Road. James Meade would be there, polishing his shoes on a Saturday night, walking through the front hall, out the path and down the Bog Road into town to Ryan's Road, for two pints and twenty woodbine, and home again to listen to the Grunow in the front kitchen, Saturday Night at the Palladium and the Goons.

Time passes. The white-faced clock with black numerals across the ward ticks, the hours ten, eleven, twelve, no one comes, no one goes, no one comes, one o'clock, lunch arrives, chicken, gravy, carrots, new boiled potatoes. Delia, finding strength, waves it away.

At two o'clock, a band comes into the ward, lining up, wearing blue and red uniforms, they begin to play their shiny wind and string instruments. At the front, a fat man beats a drum beside a thin man tapping a triangle.

There are other figures now at the bed. They may be visitors. One has blue eyes, it is the miracle child.

The band continues to play, it is not music, it is a joined-up clashing of noises, a clattering and banging and thumping, the noise drifts around the ward. Boom-boom-boom, bang-bang-bang, splash-splash, spling! Boom-boom-boom, bang-bang-bang, splash-splash, spling!

They develop a growing crescendo and somehow in their mayhem, there is a kind of uniformity, a pattern in the unevenness of it. The noise, if Delia listens carefully, is fitting together, the longer she tries to hear it, the more sense it makes, she tries to smile and feels a hair against her cheek. Everything slows down while the noise rises. The figures in front of her, Barbara and Aidan hold hands, there is whining. Others come into the ward. The three Jacks, Philly, Mary and Margaret, they look around for chairs. Joseph and Big Maureen and Small Maureen are on the other side, have they been there all the time, Delia does not know. And then she is not sure if anyone is there, anyone at all. But is it James Meade which sits opposite her? No. He is dead for years. The band has gone. Delia is alone in the ward. She is sure of that now.

The blue figure is at the bed, she puts her hand on Barbara's shoulder. Delia is trying to breathe, she is not able to breathe.

Sounds rise and fall like a muttering of birds on a summer's morning. Footsteps and low voices and coughs and doors opening and closing, the rustle of a plastic bag, the clearing of a throat, the squeeze of an intravenous drip bag, the peeling of rubber gloves. The whirring. All lie still in swivelling beds. Settling and anchoring momentarily. All turning from left to right and right to left.

Delia drifts through thoughts, thoughts appearing, thoughts of something, thoughts of anything, unable to be caught, unable to be considered.

Delia looks through the cloudy glass and tries to see the vague shapes, tries to breathe. She coughs. The air in the ward changes, becoming misty, there is something falling without moving, dislocating without progress, water surrounds Delia, dry cloudy water, filling all of the space around her, tightening her line of vision, wrapping her body, cold hard water, like liquid steel. The colours of the ward, the greys and beiges and whites are changing to no colour, to an indefinable presence and then an absence, the ward fades from Delia's vision.

Delia is cold. The blue figure takes Delia's arm, the hand colder than the air. More figures come to the bed.

There is light and dark in Delia now, cold and hot, Town and Country, now and then, she searches the void. She opens her eyes and the band has returned to the ward. Their outlines harden. They begin to play again, now the music is harmonious and pleasurable. The fat man drums, the thin man taps his triangle. The tune develops its story. Delia cannot know the story, but sees the band clearly, now in their blue and red uniforms, now in shiny brass buttons, now in polished black shoes. The chill is gone now, she feels liquid warm through her veins, her flesh, her mind. The sun comes from behind the clouds and beats down on the short grass. The carnival is busy. Delia walks with Maisie and Peggy McHale, they chatter and laugh. In the distance, there is a man in his twenties, he has a strong jawline, a squarish head, a flat stomach and broad shoulders. His white shirt is tight around his chest, his breeches hold up grey trousers over brown boots with yellow laces. He turns his head, his eyes catch Delia's.

Delia still hears the tune playing, developing into its own life, its own identity, overpowering the listener, becoming of itself more an independent thing, but then taking over the entirety, taking everything, culminating in a great and wonderful finale.

They all meet up, women and men, shake hands, Delia talks to the man, his name is James.

Sound evaporates from the ward. The grey linoleum reflects silent light. A chill wraps the air around the bed of the deceased, light touching the forms of all present.

A frost dusts the world with a vague white glow. The blue uniformed woman leaves Delia's arm gently on the blanket and nods to Barbara. Delia has stopped breathing. The blue uniformed woman closes Delia's eyes.

A man sitting at a bed across the ward comes and shakes Barbara's hand. 'Sorry ma'am.'

'Hello, who are you?'

'George Maloney, ma'am.'

'Where are you from, George?'

'The Fairways, ma'am...'

'Thanks, George. Is that your mother over there?'

'It is, ma'am.'

'What age is she?'

'Ninety. Ninety last April.'

'Thanks for coming over, George.'

Aidan scratches his beard. He stoops beside Barbara and kisses her on the cheek.

16.

They wait in the blue Kadett. They sit in the back, pulling and pushing each other. They play a slapping game, one must hit the other's hand cleanly as they touch fingertips together, palms flat, as though to pray. Three misses results in a free slap penalty. The boy is good at this game. There is a loud smack as his palm connects.

'Ow!' The girl cries. Tears drip from her eyelashes.

'Are you going to tell mam?'

'Yes. Yes I am.'

'It was only a light slap. You hit me first.'

'I don't care.'

'Come on, it was only a tap.'

'I don't care. You're a bully.'

The boy slaps the girl on the head.

'Ow! Mammy!'

'I'm not a bully! Bitch!'

Barbara and Aidan come through the entrance doors of the County Home. The boy focuses on Barbara's face, a grey smudge in the distance, the eyes and nose not visible, all he can identify clearly across the car park are the lips, tightly together in a crooked line, her head nodding as she limps on the tarmac. He knows then. Barbara and Aidan get into the Kadett. Aidan drives to Joseph's house. Nothing is said. He is relieved.

The boy stands on the edge of the car floor, his elbow on the roof, watching people around double doors. The hearse comes to a stop. Someone comes near him, a man with a moustache.

'Sorry.'

'Thanks, Paddy,' the boy says.

In the funeral home, seven of Delia's children line the walls around the coffin. Thomas and Joseph stand near two flickering candles. Sitting are: Margaret, Mary, Philly, Barbara and Kathleen, home from England for the first time in years. The boy has heard Barbara speaking of the attempts to find Sam in Australia. Joseph had made phone calls to the Irish Embassy in Canberra and to state agencies. There was no record of a Samuel Pious Meade anywhere.

Someone tells the boy to kiss Delia. He goes to the coffin, touches her hands, as he has seen others do. Delia's hands are intertwined around her rosary beads. He can see the top of the light blue cardigan she is dressed in. He kisses her forehead. It is cold and hard. The skin seems to have tightened in around the skull.

At the coffin, the boy feels nothing, then a burning, then nothing. He does not recognise Delia, he realises. Back at the wall, his eyes water, his breathing becomes stunted. He shakes a little. But it is over then.

Barbara is tear-stained, but not crying. Mary moans. Margaret and Philly whisper to each other. Kathleen stares silently at the coffin. Thomas chews tobacco. Joseph stands now on one leg, now on the other.

In the pub on Ryan's Road, Thomas drinks Bloody Marys.

'Bleddy government,' Thomas says to the barman. The three Jacks play darts. There is confusion with the similarity of their names on the scoreboard. There is a vicious argument about using their wives' names. They eventually agree to use their surnames. The boy throws a few darts. He is not very good.

The day ends and night falls. Morning comes again. The house in the Country is silent. The room where Delia slept is empty. The boy lies awake. He recalls the clay tossed down onto the coffin, covering the shine of light across the oak lid. He imagines Delia lying still underneath, her hands intertwined around her rosary beads. Her light blue cardigan. The blackness. She had looked waxen laid out, now he remembers.

'A great woman.'
   'Oh, a saint.'
   'A saint, indeed.'
   'How are ye?'
   'How are ye all?'
   'It was the crowd that are in now, they are no good.'
   'No good at all.'
   'I don't know where it'll end.'
   'There'll be no one left in this country.'
   'No. You're right, Jackie boy, you're right.'
   'Hard to see a month gone?'
   'Hard to see it.'
   'What age is Helen now? Sixteen? Did I ask you at the funeral?'
   'Gone sixteen.'

'Well. Time is flying.'

'Isn't that top nice on her?'

'She's picking her own stuff now.'

'They grow so fast.'

'They do, they do.'

The pub in Ryan's Road, empties and fills, empties and fills, a pair of eyes open and close in the gleam of the taps. The boy sits across from Thomas, wondering at the difference from when Thomas came into the bar, talking of the government, the lack of work, the bastards, and then later, to lie his head flat on the counter, his jaw slowly lifting up and down in tune with his struggled breath, saliva dripping from his mouth.

The other children of Delia sit around tables. People come and go, go and come. The boy drinks his cola, looks at Thomas asleep, now sniffing, now coughing.

'This crowd are useless.'

'Useless.'

'They should be taken out and shot.'

There is a noise from a table. Philly and Margaret each have their left hand on a glass of Harp.

'That's mine,' one says.

'That's mine,' the other says.

They pull the glass. Lager spills over their sleeves, soaking through to their arms. Someone is shouting, someone is saying, 'Calm down, calm down.'

When they get home from the pub in Ryan's Road, the boy runs around the odd shaped garden with his ball. Drizzle fades. His clothes are damp. He kicks the ball now this way, then that way, retrieves it, dribbles it, lifts it, chips it, crosses it.

'Raker, beautiful touch,' Pete Popse says. 'Elegant.'

It is morning. The boy is under his bed, lying on the brown patterned carpet amongst cardboard boxes of 'newspapers' and 'magazines'. The smell of the carpet wafts up his nose. Musty, worn. He likes it. The ground solid underneath him, underneath his whole body.

The boy walks to the bathroom, urinates in the beige toilet bowl. He looks in the mirror hanging over the sink. When he was younger, he wasn't tall enough to use it, as he grew, more and more of him filled the glass. Now he can see his eyes, his nose, his mouth, black hair. He looks at the connecting door to Barbara and Aidan's bedroom in the reflection. His eyes rest on the architrave. He slants his head to outside the line of the door frame. He washes his face with carbolic soap and dries it with the beige towel on the rail. He straightens his hair with a thick handled brush. He walks up the long hall, past his sister's bedroom and the room where Delia used to sleep. He passes through the door with the glass panel above it. In the back hall he turns toward the kitchen. He turns on the grey radio on the white counter over the washing machine, fridge and the tall compartment with Brillo pads. Morning Ireland is on.

The boy sits between the square table and the pine presses and opens the exercise book he had left there the night before. He writes 'The Morning Post' at the top of the centre page, with three decreasing lines over each word in the masthead, forming the outline of a triangle. The news bulletin comes on the hour. The main story this morning, a man killed in a car crash down the country.

A long time later, some months, the mattress Delia slept on is taken out by Aidan and burnt on the bonfire circled with stones, beside the rockery, where he gets rid of combustible waste. The mattress catches fire quickly and makes a sizzling noise as it burns. The boy watches the label sewn into the top as it peels off in the growing heat. 'Sleep right, wake up bright.'

A grid of black springs remains in the ashes later. The bed frame is left in the room, moved out from the wall, now in a diagonal position across the centre, beside the chair with the compartment underneath. The red and white marbly grooming set is on the half-moon table, until Barbara takes it away with other items. The boy doesn't think Delia ever used it.

It is evening. The boy sits on the couch in the dining room watching Home and Away on the Grundig television in the corner. To the left is the tall drinks cabinet, with drawers underneath which Barbara uses for underwear. To the right is the floor to ceiling bookcase Aidan had fitted. His sister and brother sit beside him. The door to the kitchen is ajar. The boy looks into the kitchen, at the top left-hand corner of the door which leads to the back hall. Here the architrave meets.

The boy recalls a puzzle. A box must be drawn, the top side a base for a triangle which spans across. An 'X' is drawn within the box, touching each corner. The symbol must be drawn without lifting the pen off the paper during construction. The puzzle was not difficult, he solved it quite quickly. He then tried to draw the symbol without completing the triangle on top. It was impossible. No matter how he approached it, he could not draw the box with the 'X' within in one movement. He tried it again and again.

Now he tries it here on the architrave at the intersection, using his eye line as a pen. He fails. He tries again. He fails. He watches Home and Away.

The boy sits in Barbara's yellow van outside the supermarket. The van is a Fiat 127. The previous owner had converted it, replacing the back windows with solid panels, removing the back seat, only a spare wheel now lies amongst the shadows. He likes the small steering wheel.

'Like a racing car,' Barbara said and smiled on a different day, nearly laughed. She does not smile much, does not laugh much. When she does, he feels warm.

Someone walks along the alley, past the trollies, holding a brown envelope. Barbara winds down the window.

'Hiya Bab,'

'Aright.'

'How are you, lad?'

'Fine.'

'No school, today?'

'Uh. Half day.'

'I was up at Stephens' there now, Babba, ahem…'

'Yes?'

'Well, he says it will be sold and divided…'

'What?' Barbara speaks sharply, the boy notices. A tone of someone falling off a cliff.

'That's all I know, Babba.'

'We'll see about that.'

'Look, that's what the man said.'

'I'm going.' Barbara's hand shakes as she fiddles with the keys. She starts the van. Barbara sniffs as she drives away. Someone stares after them, standing on the path, still holding the brown envelope.

Visitors call to the house in the Country. Tea is drank in the sitting room. Low voices can be heard. The three Jacks, Mary, Philly and Margaret call with their children. There is an awkwardness with the cousins now, they are older. They do not run around the odd shaped garden with the boy playing catch anymore.

Everything changes. Barbara speaks in deep tones in the kitchen later, 'annoyed' is the word he hears. The word 'Probate' is mentioned a lot, he wonders what is meant by 'Probate'. Files and folders, he sees in his imagination.

The room Delia slept in is overhauled, the frame dismantled and taken away with the tall shiny teak wardrobe. Aidan fits a shelf in the recessed area for the Grundig television. The couch from the dining room is put in the corner. It will be a living room for the children, that is what has been decided. The boy can close the door and watch television late at night, without the sound travelling to the bedrooms.

They clean out the house on the Bog Road. They had tried to renovate it for rent but had become exasperated with builders. The bathroom is full of their materials, cement bags, off cuts of timber, tiles, a still boxed shower set.

Barbara has decided to sell the house in the Bog Road, the boy hears one evening. A 'Sale Agreed' sign is placed against the glass panel over the front door.

They hoover the brown patterned carpet. They clean the tall window with newspaper. Barbara says this is the best way to clean glass. They take all the items off the red tiled mantelpiece. Aidan carries the cloth chest from the glory hole. Some items slide out as he lifts it into the Kadett. He tosses them on top and closes the boot. The photograph of Mr Flounders at the fence of the Bog Field, staring at the camera, is pressed against the glass as Aidan drives down the Bog Road to the dump.

The armchairs and the red tiled mantelpiece and the yellow patterned tiles and orange lino and the brown patterned carpet and the round table and the tall window and the drinks cabinet and the two-seater and the piano and the coat stand and everything everywhere else all remain in the house on the Bog Road.

'Just a house,' Barbara says, as she pours the contents of a green dustpan into a black bag in the front kitchen. The boy stands at the front door, looking at the number '109' while they wait for Aidan to come back and collect them. He rocks himself to sleep at night, in his bedroom in the house in the Country.

It is April. The boy walks along the field with Aidan to where the ewe lies. Clouds crowd the sky. The grass is wet. Aidan walks ahead of him, as though in a hurry. The ewe lies on her back.

Every day this time of year the boy is sent out to check if any sheep are lying on their back, as their fleeces get thicker. If they are left more than a few hours, they will die. This one he missed.

The sheep is bloated, a huge white ball of stillness. They begin to dig, stones in the ground block the boy's spade. Soil comes out in wet lumps. Deeper they dig. The hole sufficient, they turn the sheep in. They cover her over with the sods of earth. Aidan taps the topping down.

The boy looks back at the brown patch in the field as they walk away, imagining the sheep underneath, thinking of the insects that will come and eat through the decomposing flesh. Aidan has walked over to the stone wall.

'Come over here, we'll build a few of these back up,' he says.

Every evening the three of them watch Home and Away at half six in the room where Delia used to sleep. Often, the boy looks at the top corner of the door where the architrave meets and he tries to draw the square with the 'X' within, using his eye line as a pen. Although he knows it is impossible, he tries it again and again.

Still the fridge hums in the corner. The beige linoleum has lifted at the edges. The wallpaper remains, fading now, of Mickey Mouse, Donald Duck and Goofy. They argue about a toy train. They each have a paw placed on it. On the ceiling, the poster of the kitten tucked under the pink blanket has curled at one corner, where the Blu-tack has fallen off.

Over weeks and months, the room becomes called the TV Room, or the Living Room, or even the Kids' Room. Sometimes Barbara calls it Mammy's Room, but the boy notices that this is rare. He still calls it Gran's Room, for a while at least.

The boy never goes to the grave of Delia, and he never goes back again to the Bog Road. He sits on the couch, late at night with the door closed, watching the Grundig television, looking up at the architrave now and then, hearing the fridge hum.

In the odd shaped garden, the boy runs around, up and down the gentle slope, near the rock, kicking the ball against the two foot bank near the hedge. The hedge Aidan preserved as it was part of the field before ever the house was built in the Country. The boy kicks the ball high into the air. It bounces against the two electrical cables which run across the pitch in the stadium as it falls. He traps the ball as it lands, turns and scores, 'A great goal by the striker, this man has class,' Pete Popse says.

The boy's team has won the final. He walks off the odd shaped garden, across the drive, up to the windowsill outside Barbara and Aidan's bedroom where the trophy will be presented. His team walk up before him to collect their medals. They laugh and joke as they always do on these occasions.

As captain, the boy is presented finally with the trophy, a broken relic of a sports day. He holds it over his head to cheers. He walks back to the pitch with his team. They all do a lap of honour around the stadium, applauding the crowd.

Later, he will place the trophy inside, on the window board of his bedroom, but the celebrations will be all over by then.

Delia Meade is Martin Keaveney's debut novel. His debut short story collection, *The Rainy Day*, was published in 2018 by Penniless Press. Stage and screen credits include Ireland's national broadcaster RTE and Scripts Ireland Playwriting Festival. He has a PhD in Creative Writing and Textual Studies. Scholarship has been published widely, including at the *New Hibernia Review, Journal of Franco-Irish Studies* and *Estudios Irlandeses*. He was awarded the Sparanacht Ui Eithir for his research in 2016. He works as a creative writing lecturcr/consultant (see more at *www.martinkeaveney.com*).

THE RAINY DAY

Farmers: young and old, cunning, foolish, greedy, generous, talented and forgotten. These and those belonging to them are gathered in this short story collection, sometimes clearly in Ireland's west, but mostly in an unnamed landscape which shapes those often waiting for that rainy day to come. It was published by Penniless Press in 2019.

'*The Rainy Day* […] will really strike a chord with rural readers.'

Connaught Telegraph

Purchase *The Rainy Day* at www.mayobooks.ie

www.ingramcontent.com/pod-product-compliance
Lightning Source LLC
Chambersburg PA
CBHW060424260626
47161CB00005B/1768